2.00

**W9-AAS-651**

# A COOLER CLIMATE

## ZENA COLLIER

BRITISH AMERICAN PUBLISHING, LTD.

My special thanks to the
Virginia Center for the Creative Arts
where most of this novel was written

Copyright 1990 by Zena Collier
All rights reserved
including the right of reproduction
in whole or in part in any form.
Published by British American Publishing
3 Cornell Road
Latham, NY 12110
Manufactured in the United States of America

94  93  92  91  90  5  4  3  2  1

Library of Congress Cataloging-in-Publication Data

Collier, Zena, 1926–
    A cooler climate / Zena Collier.
      p.  cm.
    ISBN 0-945167-29-6
    I. Title.
PR6069.H75C66   1990
823'.914—dc20                                              89–28352
                                                              CIP

*For Eleanor*
*And in memory of Jeff*

# 1

"HAVE YOU TALKED TO HER?" Nat spoke in the garbled mumble which meant he was lighting his pipe.

"Talked!" In my mind's eye, I saw Joanna, chewing nicotine gum because she'd given up cigarettes yet again. "Till I'm blue in the face. For all the good it does."

Their conversation came up the heating ducts as clearly as though it were taking place right here in the bedroom. This dialogue wasn't news. I was well aware that Joanna had lost patience with me. She'd told me so, outright. "Iris, I cannot understand this desire to reduce yourself to the lowest common denominator."

"As I see it, I'm trying to get by."

She had sighed. "We've been over and over this. You're intelligent, Iris, but your feet simply aren't on the ground."

I'd had a vision of myself then, floating Mary Poppins-like a tidy distance above terra firma. All very well for Joanna; Joanna was supported by a husband, and she also earned a salary at teaching which could, if worst came to worst, enable her to take care of herself. Joanna had had the foresight years ago to make sure she had formal qualifications.

"She's leaving for Maine tomorrow?" I heard Nat ask.

"So she says." There was a dull thud, as though Joanna had banged down a book. "I wish I could stop her."

"Well, you've done everything possible. Nothing more we can do, if her mind's made up. She's an adult, after all."

1

An adult. I was forty-five according to the calendar, but lately I'd begun to feel like that woman who, leaving Shangri-La, grew years older by the minute. Each time I looked in a mirror, I was surprised to see it wasn't so; I might feel bent and gnarled, bowed over by the weight of problems, but the mirror showed a person of reasonably upright carriage, with dark hair still untouched by grey and deep-set, rather heavy-lidded eyes which gave—Oliver had once said—a look of hauteur. Color in my cheeks attested to general health and sturdiness. I was capable-looking, too, no matter how less than capable I seemed to be lately.

"That son-of-a-bitch," Joanna said.

"Oh, I don't think Oliver—"

"Not Oliver. Harry. More money than he knows what to do with—"

"Iris signed that agreement."

"Her lawyer was incompetent. No responsible lawyer would have let her sign such a document."

"She was in a hurry. She didn't stop to think. Anyone with half an eye could have told her Oliver wasn't reliable."

"That's hindsight."

"Maybe. Still, there's no denying she's much too impulsive. Always has been. She should have thought twice before she walked out on Harry. Or at least she should have handled it differently."

"Perhaps. Caution's never been her strong suit."

It wasn't only from Joanna I'd heard that feet-on-the-ground bit. Everyone I knew had expressed surprise at my latest plan. No one seemed to understand that I no longer had any choice. Why couldn't they understand? Was it because I was still wearing clothes left from my palmy days with Harry, so didn't actually look *in extremis?* All these accusations about not being in touch with reality. Reality had directed me to sell my jewelry some time ago. More recently, when my car developed major problems, reality had dictated I sell the car as well. I'd hated to let the car go and had nearly called Joanna to ask for a loan for repairs. But I hadn't, finally. I already owed Joanna a lot of money. I'd borrowed from a number of other people, too, none of whom I could bear to approach still again. Besides, everyone I asked for money felt obliged to deliver a homily along with the requested sum. "But Iris, you shouldn't be having this problem. You're awfully bright. You can do lots of things."

So I had thought. I'd held on to that illusion far too long. It wasn't enough to be able to turn out a perfect *vitello tonnato* and give all those dinner parties for friends and for Harry and his colleagues in plastic surgery. It wasn't enough to work as a volunteer on the orchestra drive, or sing in the oratorio society, or help a friend hang shows in her gallery. It wasn't enough to run a house all those years and raise a child who was now a thriving, upwardly mobile professional—a lawyer, no less. (No heart, but that was another matter.)

Illusion, yes. At first, the anguish I felt when Oliver left me had obscured the grim economic facts. For a while it had been all I could do to get out of bed each morning and struggle through the day, let alone try to formulate some plan for the future. Only gradually had I come to the bitter realization that Joanna had been right when she urged me to take more time negotiating the settlement with Harry. "Think of the long run," Joanna kept saying. It had never occurred to me to hedge my bets, to devise Plan B in case Plan A came to naught—Plan A, life with Oliver, had seemed so firmly in place, sworn to, entrenched.

Eventually I had pulled myself together and cast about for employment. I did find jobs, but something invariably went wrong each time. The development job at the museum lasted barely two months; raising money wasn't my strength, apparently. The job with the interior decorator didn't work out either—it seemed I acceded too easily to clients' preferences. Working in the crafts shop was pleasant, but how could anyone be expected to live on what they paid? After that, I had taken the final installment of Harry's lump-sum settlement, and launched a second-hand designer-label clothing boutique, Twice Around. Twice Around hardly went once around before it grew clear I wasn't cut out to be an entrepreneur. Oh, why, instead of living blindly in the lap of false security all these years, unaware as any perfumed poppet in a seraglio, why hadn't I bothered to acquire marketable skills?

It was after this last debacle that my real panic had begun. By now, it wasn't only my money that was gone. My self-confidence, too, had vanished. I needed not just to work, but to find some kind of work I was sure I could handle.

It was in this frame of mind that I had come across the advertisement in the Help Wanted section. The more I studied it, the more I became convinced that it might be the answer.

I told no one else about it at first. I wrote to the box number, and when I received an answer, went resolutely to the appointment at what turned out to be an employment agency.

There I was shown into an office where a large woman with rouged cheeks gave me an appraising stare, waved me to the chair across from her, and proceeded to study the form I'd filled out. That form! Backward reeled the mind, one's entire life flashed by with all major mistakes and omissions underlined in red.

"You're forty-five, Mrs. Prue?"

"Yes." I'd hesitated before writing it down, wondering whether I dared shave off a few years, but decided ultimately that lying would only make me nervous.

She looked at me hard, and I felt relieved that I'd told the truth: this person could obviously ferret out false information as easily as a Geiger counter could detect radioactivity.

4

"You look younger." Her tone was accusatory. "We were specifically asked for someone mature."

"Oh." I slumped a little, allowed my back to become rounded, placed both hands squarely on my handbag, and crossed my feet at the ankles in an elderly way, wishing my pumps were sensible oxfords. "Forty-five is hardly the heyday of youth," I pleaded.

"You're single?"

"Divorced, yes."

"No encumbrances, I take it?"

"Encumbrances?"

"Dependents. Children or—"

"Only my daughter. She's twenty-five. Not dependent." My daughter seemed to think I was *her* encumbrance.

"Two years of college?"

"Er—not quite two years."

I'd been halfway through my sophomore year when I'd met Harry, all those years ago. He'd been about to leave for a year's fellowship in England. "Marry me! We'll honeymoon in the Cotswolds!" His blue eyes had gleamed, his narrow face had flamed with ardor. Without hesitation I had placed myself in his custody and left college. My parents didn't seriously object. In those days, most people, including my parents, still believed that the only really suitable career for a woman was marriage. And both my mother and my father— an underpaid English professor at a small Midwestern college—were impressed by Harry, who would obviously provide well and who had trotted out the charm he kept on tap for special occasions.

The woman's gaze raked me from head to toe. "Do you think you're really suited for this kind of work? You're not exactly a typical applicant."

"I know I can do it. I've been doing it for much of my life, after all."

"But under somewhat different circumstances."

I leaned forward, urgent. "I assure you, I really need—"

"Yes, but will you stick with it, that's the question. Our clients pay the fee, they expect us to send—"

"I understand. I wouldn't have come if I weren't serious."

Lengthy pause.

"Well, I'll give you the details," she said. "Then, if you're still interested, you'll have to go up to Maine for an interview. Our client will pay for bus transportation."

With Hurdle One negotiated, I had taken the bus northward, where I successfully negotiated Hurdle Two. I rode back to Boston feeling elated. I had achieved *something*, finally. A real job, at last.

Still feeling triumphant, I called Joanna to tell her. She greeted my announcement with total silence.

"Joanna? Are you there?"

"*Housekeeper?* You must be insane! Look, I can lend you—"

"No, Joanna, though I'm grateful. That's no solution, only a temporary respite. Anyway, I won't need it now. That's the point."

"But—why this?"

"Why? It's a job."

"It's so—" She stopped.

Joanna, don't do this, I pleaded silently, don't make me feel I've made still another mistake.

"—demeaning."

"Honest work for honest pay is the way I see it."

"Iris, be reasonable!"

"What could be more reasonable? I'll have wages, food on the table, a roof over my head. What's more," I added, "I'll be living by the sea!"

That last was intended as a lighter touch, but of all the material benefits I'd given up when I left my marriage, it was the cottage at Wellfleet that I missed most of all. To be within sight and sound of the ocean was life-giving, restorative. When I'd heard the location of this job, it had struck me as an auspicious omen.

"Iris, this is the twentieth century! You don't have to go off and be a servant, for God's sake!"

"Don't be ridiculous," I said, irritably.

"*I'm* ridiculous?" She gave a raucous hoot.

I'd tried to forget it, but Joanna's reaction, plus some inner flutterings of my own, had done their work even while I sold off my furniture, gave up my apartment, and cast myself on Joanna and Nat's hospitality for the few days remaining before I was due to start work.

As I lay sleepless now in their guest bedroom, I suddenly felt chilled. My teeth began to chatter. What on earth—? Then I realized: fear, like a monstrous crab, had seized me in its horrid grip and would not let me go.

# 2

FEAR STAYED WITH ME for a long time. It became almost panic as I said goodbye to Joanna at the bus station. It rode with me as we rumbled along the highway. At Portland, where I changed buses, it suddenly left me—why, I can't say. Perhaps one can only sustain fear—like joy or anger or any extreme emotion—for a limited time. Or perhaps, as everyone implied, I was indeed lacking in stability, and therefore incapable of sustaining *any* emotion. So, as in the past I had run out of happiness, run out of confidence, run out of money, this time I had run out of fear. It was replaced by a fatalism which spoke with a calm voice: You've taken the plunge. Now we'll see.

The sun was shining, but the nascent green of the New England countryside grew less evident as we rode further north. At Portland it was cooler than it had been in Boston on this late spring day. It would be cooler still where I was going. A different climate, for a different life.

The last part of the journey was strange. We were late leaving Portland; about a dozen of us sat in the bus for twenty minutes before the driver boarded. A portly man, he breathed heavily as he settled himself behind the wheel. For several minutes he pored over a map. Finally, muttering, he started the bus, swung the wheel, and drove out of the station. As he did so, he made an announcement. "I'm just filling in for a guy who's sick. This ain't my route."

9

Nor mine, either. Nor had anyone given me even a map. I would have to find my own way.

As we approached each town, he slowed and appealed to us for directions. Unorthodox routes were proposed and followed. "Hang a right here and cut across the tracks." "Turn left at the church, I'll get out at the gas station." "Take the bridge over the creek and let me off at the fruit stand."

At last we arrived. "Staunton," the driver announced, and mopped his brow.

Again, as when I'd come for the interview, my employer was waiting in the bottle-green Porsche.

"You're late," was her greeting.

"Yes, the driver—"

"Put your things in the trunk. I'm in a hurry. My husband's calling from Paris at four."

Mrs. Tanner. Paula. Was she fifty? More? Hard to say. She must once have been breathtakingly lovely, was handsome now in a manufactured way—aided, I suspected, by one of Harry's brethren. Her face looked unnaturally smooth, almost polished, beneath the blonde hair drawn tightly back from a flawless forehead. I'd had the impression at our first meeting that she towered above me, but I realized now that in fact she was barely an inch taller.

I disliked her from the very start—cold, arrogant, spoiled, I thought her. My judgment could hardly be unbiased, of course; there I was, needy, with figurative cap in hand; there she was, with power to assuage or ignore that need—a power that seemed to increase with every mile we drove towards the house.

That house. If you approached from the hill and looked down, it seemed incongruous, a series of tall, joined, up-ended boxes out on the point. But as you drove through the woods and came on it up close, you saw that it was exactly right, it was perfect. The shape, thrusting upward among the cedars and spruce, and the color, a greenish-grey echoing the ocean, kept it beautifully in harmony with the setting.

At ground level it was half-surrounded by a sundeck. Two of the upstairs rooms had decks of their own from which could be seen not only the woods, the garden, the contoured pool, but the low bluffs and the crescent of gravel beach studded with rocks ranging from ochre through peach to black. And finally, there was the sea, in its transcendent majesty, crashing forcefully against the rocks or demurely sliding around their crannies as the tide receded.

"We don't swim in the ocean, it's much too cold," she had told me at the interview. "You may use the pool any time, of course."

She had led me briskly through the house. "Here's the dining room, though mostly we eat outdoors when we can, weather and black flies permitting. When it's just Leo and me, we eat here in the breakfast room"—a sunny area just off the kitchen. In the living room, a vast expanse of snowy white rug covered the floor; sofas and chairs were slipcovered in white linen. "A disaster. You see the problem." I saw. There'd been a plumbing mishap during the winter while the house was closed; the ceiling had collapsed, the wall had crumbled, the wooden floor was warped and mildewed and much of the rug was ruined. This was why she had arrived early, ahead of the season; workmen would shortly start on repairs and redecorating. "If I'm not here to keep an eye on them, heaven knows how it'll turn out." Her husband was a lawyer with a theatrical practice. The walls of his study were lined with framed, inscribed photographs. In that three-second glimpse, I recognized a legendary director and an actress considered the grande dame of American theatre. "This is *my* hideaway . . ." Bamboo furniture in white, a white typewriter, again a white rug. Bedrooms on the second floor. On the third floor, across the hallway from my quarters, was another bedroom. "This is Beth's room, my daughter's. She's seldom here, however." For an instant something crossed her face, then vanished.

Everything throughout the house was white, or palest pale.

Everywhere showed the fine, dead hand of the decorator. All was immaculate—not a speck or smudge or worn spot anywhere.

Downstairs, she opened a door. "Cleaning supplies." Here was an incredible array of mops, brooms, electric polishers, sweepers, all displayed and labeled like museum exhibits. I didn't know whether I admired or was repelled by this triumph of efficiency. I was resigned to the fact that "housekeeper, some cooking" encompassed all the housework, but was I up to these sterile standards? In this setting the slightest trace of grime, the smallest object out of place, would stand out like bloodstains at the scene of a murder.

Still, I would do my best. There were compensations, after all. The ocean. And those quarters on the third floor—not just a room but an entire suite of my own: living room, bedroom, kitchenette, bathroom. The rose-dappled bedspread and curtains, the beige rug and paisley print sofa, might be leftovers banished by decorator's edict, but the general effect was pleasing and comfortable. In my living room were shelves crammed with books—"Leo's overflow. They can go in the storage room if they're in your way"—also television and radio. A small desk by the living-room window leaned slightly askew. "We'll get that fixed when Leo comes. He enjoys doing that sort of thing—repairs, gardening, cooking occasionally. It helps him unwind."

"Well, unpack and get settled." She flashed a smile that seemed superimposed like a stage moustache, disappearing as quickly as it came. "Then come down to the kitchen. I opened your windows, but you'd better close them. It looks like rain."

My own little kitchen was stocked with tea, coffee, milk, and other staples. There was a telephone and intercom. On the slightly peeling rattan coffee table stood a small, crystal jug filled with the special blue of grape hyacinths—a kind touch, I wouldn't have expected it, somehow.

My spirits lifted. Look upon it as an adventure, I thought. I slid my emptied suitcase under the bed, then placed a framed snapshot of Callie on my bureau, beside my travel alarm clock.

For a moment I stood by the window, looking down on the woods. From here I couldn't see the ocean, but I could smell it, the scent of ozone mingling with the scent of pine and cedar. While I unpacked, the sky had turned the color of steel, the mewling of gulls sounded like cries of warning.

Suddenly doubt rushed in—leave, get out, it's all a mistake!

Stop that, I told myself firmly, closed the windows, and went down the back stairs—servant's stairs?—that led directly to the kitchen.

Here, too, all was white, pristine. Nothing suggested habitation except, just now, a pot of coffee on the stove.

Paula Tanner sat at the table, writing something. "Find everything you need?"

"Thank you, yes."

"Pour us coffee, please, while I finish this. I take mine black. Cups over there." She went on writing.

Thank heaven for the coffee; it meant automatically that I could—must—sit down with her. This was the hardest part, the question of how I was supposed to comport myself. Certain things had been made implicitly clear: I wouldn't take my meals with her, or them, unless specifically invited to do so. And she was to be "Mrs. Tanner" to me, not "Paula." (So far she had dodged what I was to be by not calling me anything at all.) But what, for example, was I supposed to wear? A frilly white apron and cap, such as one saw in French farce? Or an amorphous disguising black dress, such as worn by evil Mrs. Danvers in *Rebecca?* Other rules had been spelled out: I was to use the station wagon for errands, never the Porsche, and I must always ask before using the wagon for personal use; whenever I used the wagon for myself, I would, of course, buy my own gasoline. My hours would vary, depending on the season. At present I was free weekday evenings, Wednesday afternoons, and all day Sundays. As summer advanced, I'd have less time off. "Soon, Leo will be here for weekends. In July and August he'll be here most of the time. His clients are marvellous but difficult. He has to get away. This place is his refuge." In the past the Tanners had closed the house after Labor Day, but since the plumbing disaster they had decided someone should stay here over the winter. This had been another inducement to take the job; whatever summer was like, I'd have the place to myself come September.

"I'm writing out a list of places where you'll shop. Burdick's in Staunton for fruits and vegetables. Captain Bligh's on the wharf for—" Suddenly, she put down the pen. "This won't work."

"I have a pen—"

"No. I mean this. *You.*" She gestured at me. "I'm sorry," she said, in a different voice. "I should have realized—"

"Realized?"

"It isn't feasible, you being here—"

"You mean, you don't want me?" Dismay tuned my voice to an anxious treble.

"I can't exactly see myself telling you to do a better job on the bathrooms or—"

"Why not? I'm perfectly able—"

"It's not a question of you being able. It's a matter of my not feeling comfortable. I had doubts as soon as we met. Why someone like you would want—"

"I thought I explained—"

"You said you were divorced, and without resources. But I still don't see—"

"Does it matter? So long as I do the work properly?" To be fired before I had even begun!

She stroked her throat absently. A square emerald on her ring finger caught the light. Those well-kept hands showed a number of brown spots. I myself had a couple. Oliver had touched them gently, looking thoughtful, then turned my hand over and pressed his lips to the palm.

"I'm sorry. I'll pay your expenses, of course, for return transportation and also—"

Return to what? "*Please*. I promise you won't find it difficult."

"But—"

"I've burned all my bridges, you see."

She studied me critically. "It sounds as though you don't know how to look after yourself."

"I'm trying to learn," I said, humbly. A refuge, yes, at the edge of the sea. Blessed, mindless work, therapeutic. Held safe, no worries.

"How long were you married?"

Surprised, I had to think before answering. "Twenty-three years."

She looked away, towards the windows. "I had my thirty-first anniversary in April."

There but for the grace, did she mean? I held my breath.

The sound of the telephone broke the silence. She stood so quickly that a little of the coffee spilled. "That'll be Paris. Pick it up, tell them to hold, I'll take it in my study."

# 3

THERE ARE TIMES in your life, pivotal stages and events, on which you can look back later and see, as easily as though reading a map, just where you went wrong. For me, these wrong turnings all seemed to result from forgetting or flouting some cardinal rule often stated in terms of a shopworn axiom: Marry in haste, repent at leisure. Look before you leap. Moderation in all things.

My first major error at the Tanners was that promise I gave, which was bound to make my life burdensome. I forgot about *start as you mean to go on*. Of course, someone more secure than Paula wouldn't have taken it so literally, wouldn't have insisted on keeping me to it. But I wasn't to know her situation.

As the days passed and I moved around those rooms, sweeping, dusting, washing, polishing, it took a while before the ramifications of my new position were borne in on me. It grew clear almost at once that the work itself wouldn't be a problem. The work required only physical energy, and there was something almost soothing about the mechanical, repetitive tasks. Not for years had I done heavier chores, such as washing paintwork or cleaning windows, but now I tackled these and more without turning a hair. At night, dead tired from these labors, I fell asleep at once without thinking about anything—not money, not the past, not Callie, not Oliver.

Oliver. Despite everything, I still missed him . . . and yes, yearned for him. I felt like one of those Henry Moore sculptures, those figures done in sections that don't quite join; whether I would ever grow back together again, becoming whole and entire, was doubtful.

But the work was all right, the work in fact seemed just what I needed.

Dealing with the lady of the house, however, was another matter. For example, when a room looked impeccable, I naturally assumed there was nothing to be done. Wrong. She wanted certain rooms turned out daily, even if they were totally unsullied by human presence. This seemed to me pointless, but I fixed on a strategy of low profile at all times— don't question, follow orders, eyes straight ahead. Obedient and silent as any robot, I washed the kitchen windows on Mondays, changed linens Tuesdays and Fridays, and daily swept from the deck the handful of twigs that had the temerity to land there. She said it troubled her that she had to—as she put it—"spell out every detail." She claimed the problem arose because I hadn't done this kind of work before on a paid basis. I could hardly say, "The problem is you're anal-compulsive."

It took me a while to realize we were engaged in a contest: she was determined to show she wasn't going to treat me differently from anyone else she might have hired; I was equally determined to show I was willing and able not only to do the work, but to be as faceless as any cipher. Towards the end of my second week, I was in the kitchen mopping the floor when she entered. Here it came: "That's all right for touch-ups, Iris—" quick-flick smile—"but once a week I want the floor scrubbed, please." Down on my hands and knees I went, with bucket and brush. It didn't bother me, but oddly I think it bothered *her*. She stayed away for hours after that, almost as though she were hiding.

As the days passed, she tended to give fewer instructions face to face; more often her voice issued, depersonalized, metallicized, from the intercom. *Iris, I wish*, was the way these communications began. "Iris, I wish you'd give my blouse another touch with the iron. The cuffs need attention." "Iris, I wish you'd wipe off the telephones regularly. I don't like to see fingerprints." "Iris, I wish you'd clean up pots right away, not let them stand."

At times, I longed to swear and fling the broom at her, but then I'd recall my ill-fated ventures of the past. The decorator, for example, Belisario, with the accent and features of a Tuscan prince. "Iris, I like you personally very much, but—" he had spread his hands—"I cannot any longer afford you! How shall I make money if you discourage Mrs. Gregory from her intentions to decorate her music room?"

"Discourage Mina? I didn't. She decided to go ahead with the bedrooms but she didn't think she wanted—"

"And you told her she was right, no? Leave it alone, this room is perfect as it is, you told her. This she tells me when I go to show her the plans."

"But—"

"Iris, I know you are friend of Mrs. Gregory. This is why I give you the job, your connections. But if you work for me, you do not work as friend of Mrs. Gregory, all the Mrs. Gregorys. You work for Belisario, to increase my business, earn your salary."

"Of course. I realize that."

"No, Iris, I think you do not. You treat this work as— what shall I say? A hobby." He had shaken his head with such regret that it had taken me a moment to realize I was fired.

Wherein lay the key to this woman's character, I wondered. A silver-framed photograph on the piano showed her in what seemed to be her early thirties. Despite the thin plucked eyebrows and rigid pageboy of that era, she was pretty, laughing as the shutter clicked, white teeth straight as soldiers. No clues, though. There were lots of chichi magazines around and shiny bestsellers immaculate as virgins, but I had yet to see her read. The only books that looked as though they served their purpose were the ones in his study and his discards in my living room, which ranged from Lorenz on aggression to Leonard Feather on jazz to what seemed to be a first edition of *Kitty Foyle*—a mistake, surely, consigning a first edition to Siberia? I said nothing about it, however; I mustn't seem to be questioning her knowledge or judgment. At all times I had to take care not to say or do anything which suggested I might be her peer.

In the evenings, she mostly watched television and did crewel work. I'd usually be summoned to bring her a drink, coffee, whatever. If there was someone on she knew from the Wide World of Entertainment, she would graciously honor me with a comment. "That's Leo's client. He's been in several plays by—oh, what is his name, the South African playwright . . ." I sensed that if I forgot myself and supplied the name, and told her I'd seen two of those plays, my tenure would be in jeopardy. I could only nod and look impressed, and perhaps add in a tone of respectful interest, "Is that so?"

But as the days and then weeks went by, another, more serious, problem grew evident: I was lonely. I can't say precisely what I'd imagined when I took this job. I think I'd pictured a house filled with sunshine and the sound of the sea, talk, activity, comings and goings. I'd be in the midst of a hub of interesting people. Naturally, I wouldn't expect to be part of their circle, but there'd be a normal amount of civil interchange. I hadn't expected this Ice Palace with the Ice Queen herself in charge. I hadn't foreseen that she'd rarely address me, except about the work. Nor had it occurred to me that I might have difficulty getting to know people outside the house.

Only now did I realize that the only people who lived

close by were our neighbors on the cove, and these—a movie mogul, a prominent publisher, a State Department biggie, and so forth—weren't likely to extend their friendship to the Tanners' maid. I had no lines to the visitors occupying the motels and more modest cottages. Who was left?

In desperation, I searched for activities where I might be admitted to the human race, but so far there wasn't a great deal available: free knife-sharpening at the seniors' center didn't draw me, nor did the selectmen's meeting on illegal night fishing; a tofu workshop held little appeal. Finally, I ventured forth to an evening of square dancing at the Methodist church. There I learned, the hard way, that the natives didn't fraternize.

Gradually I became aware that, though her situation was vastly different from mine, Paula, too, was very much alone here. The Tanners had had this place for several years, but no one except service people seemed to come by. Paula departed in tennis whites twice weekly for the club, but no partner ever showed up at the house. Had she no friends? It was true that this was only the end of May, so most of the people she knew wouldn't yet have arrived; things would probably change for her in a month or so.

Meanwhile, the two of us rattled around that house like castaways on a desert island. We should have been company for each other in our common predicament, but because she was from first class and I was from steerage, we mustn't communicate, we might only eye each other warily.

On Friday afternoon of the first weekend in June, I sat at my desk writing to Joanna: *All week, we had been waiting for Godot. I had ironed his Egyptian cotton pyjamas; I had cleaned every inch of his study; I had memorized his breakfast preferences—unstrained orange juice (she prefers strained), croissants, marmalade, Colombian coffee (she takes Jamaican). Then came a call to say he had to stay in New York, after all, for the*

*opening of a client's show. So she's gone there instead. I drove
her to the airport this morning . . .*

As I wrote, the plaintive, dreamlike sound of a bell buoy
floated in through the window. Fog had shut down an hour
earlier; I could barely make out the tops of the trees, which
stirred occasionally like mythic creatures moving in slumber.

*. . . I'm curious about the Prince Consort, legal advisor to
the stars, alias Mr. Fix-It. Will he be steely-eyed, raspy-voiced,
barking out orders? Squat, paunchy, bald, with ubiquitous cigar?
He'll soon be here much of the time. Houseguests, too. But no
large parties, she says. "Leo comes here to escape all that." True?
I can only hope.*

Again the mournful sound of the buoy, haunting, obsessive.
Suddenly, my elation at being on my own left me. I longed
for the sight of another human presence, the sound of a
voice to counteract that feeble wail. Someone, anyone. The
workmen? But they had left early. I was alone. Around me
the silence of the house thickened, like the fog.

Are you mad? She's gone! You don't have to sit here!

Of course! I'd take the station wagon and drive into Staunton. The restaurants would mostly still be closed, the hand-
lettered sign would still be on the door of the tiny Regent
Theatre—"Oldies and Goodies! Grand Opening July 4th! Free
popcorn!"—but I'd find something, some friendly light in an
open establishment, be it only a bar or a greasy spoon.

*Signing off. Join us next week for the further adventures of
Iris Prue, Madcap Maid! Will she be fumbled in the laundry?
Tumbled in the pantry? Discharged and sent on her way, weeping,
by the Lady of the Manor? Stay tuned!*

I exchanged my jeans for fresh corduroys, my plaid shirt
for blouse and sweater, closed the windows, locked up the
house, and took off.

A diligent search yielded only Sandy's Legal Beverages.
The juke box in there was crazy-loud, I could hear the high-

pitched clamor of country and western while I was still outside parking. Never mind, it was better than nothing.

Inside, several men sat at the bar. The few formica-topped tables were empty. Plastic signs advertising beer, pretzels, potato chips, cigarettes, hung above the bar; among them, a long-legged, pointy-bosomed fantasy dolly smiled down from a 1956 Petty Girl calendar. The dour, almost toothless bartender could himself have modeled for a Down East calendar. When I approached, the men fell silent. I felt both uneasy and impatient; hadn't they ever seen a woman in a bar before? Or was it because I was a stranger?

"Yes, chablis is fine." I raised my voice to be heard over the juke box. The bartender turned down the volume slightly. The men resumed talking as I carried my drink over to a table. I studied a sign on the wall that listed sandwiches. When I went back to order, one of the men spoke. "This your night out?"

I was about to deliver a snappy retort when I recognized him. Purple-faced, bulbous-nosed, he looked different without the white cap which had "Captain Bligh's" emblazoned across it.

The second time I'd gone to his store to buy fish, he had tilted the cap back on his head and announced loudly, as though I were deaf, "Name's Spigott. Fred. I'm a widower." *Chop.* His knife had neatly severed the head of a salmon. "Got a nice little place over to Bosseyville. Ought to come over some evening and see it—wall-to-wall carpet, aluminum siding, picture windows."

Was he looking for a date or a house-buyer? I told him my evenings weren't free.

"You married? I don't see no ring." His squirrelly eyes fixed on me suspiciously.

"I work evenings."

"At the Tanners?" My purchases were charged on their account, so he knew I lived there. "You his secretary?"

"Housekeeper."

"Housekeeper, huh? I thought you were a secretary or something."

After that, his manner had become matey. He'd told me off-color jokes and nudged me to make sure I got them. Still, he was harmless, I thought. Probably lonely, in the house with wall-to-wall carpeting. His wife had died the previous summer. "Her sister Nan moved in at the end to take care of her. Nan's a good woman, but I wasn't sorry to see her leave. A man needs his privacy." He winked. "Get me?"

He followed now as I took my sandwich back to the table. "Buy you a drink?"

"Thank you, I've reached my limit."

"What you been up to?" He sat down heavily.

"Not much."

"I'm remodeling. You ought to drop by, see how I'm doing. Going to get me a new refrigerator, stainless steel sink, new cabinets . . ."

I sat there, letting his voice run on. Even if I'd wanted to, I couldn't have gotten a word in edgeways. Perhaps if life continued this way, I would gradually lose the faculty of speech, except for certain key phrases—"We're out of bags for the vacuum cleaner." "Shall I do the other bathrooms?" "What time would you like dinner?"

I was rescued by the jukebox, which was now blasting forth again. "I can't hear you," I shouted.

Looking peeved, he left me finally and went back to the bar.

I turned the key in the door, then stopped, reluctant to go forward into the emptiness. At last I forced myself to enter. In the kitchen I poured myself a glass of wine from an open bottle in the refrigerator. Then I marched from room to room, switching on lights. In the living room, I sat down at the grand piano—huge and white, like something from a Busby Berkeley musical—and played a few bars of a Bach sonata. The notes seemed to curl around me, enclosing me delicately until they faded, releasing me once more to inhospitable silence. In the dining room, I sat at the head of the table and pumped my foot rhythmically on the floor buzzer that sounded in the kitchen. *No one's in the kitchen with Iris,* I sang, *No one's in the kitchen I knoooow . . .*

In her study I sat at her desk and studied an eight-by-ten blow-up of a young woman with bushy hair and a sulky expression—Beth, the daughter. I rolled a sheet of paper into her typewriter. *Dear Oliver,* I typed with two fingers, *Who needs you, anyway?*

In his study I sat in his swivel chair and looked through a pamphlet on his desk, *Law seminars: Negotiating Contracts in the Entertainment Industry.* His name headed the list of faculty. I swung around, examining the photographs displayed on the wall. "To Leo, who kept me going through the big project." "For Leo, a real wise guy." "Leo, counsellor and friend . . ." "Leo the lion-hearted." He'd have to be, to spend thirty years with *her.*

The telephone rang.

I picked up, smartly. "Tanner residence!"

"Iris? How are things going?"

The boss lady, checking up.

"Everything's fine."

"Is it? I called earlier and got no answer."

"I went out."

"Oh."

Disapproval reverberated in that single syllable. Was I supposed to just sit here, then, like Patience on a monument?

"That's perfectly all right, of course, but lock up carefully when you go out. And leave a few lights burning. Well, intermission's nearly over, I'd better get back. I called because I've changed my flight. Meet me at four o'clock, please, on Monday."

"I'll be there."

I could hear a buzz of voices in the background, could

visualize the first-night crowd spilling from the lobby to stand beneath the marquee in the warm, polluted city air, their talk incessant as the chirp of crickets in a downy meadow.

That night I dreamed I paid a visit to the house where I'd lived with Harry. Harry still lived there, in fact, with someone who was a lab technician.

In my dream I knocked at the door which still bore the brass doorknocker we'd found in Florence, shaped like the head of a Roman centurion. A young woman opened the door. Her flaxen hair hung in two long braids. I smiled to set her at ease. "I'm Iris Prue. I'd like to see Dr. Prue, please."

She looked doubtful. "You have an appointment?"

*Haf an appointment.* German? Swiss?

"Certainly. I'm here about a job."

"Job?" She looked flustered. "You come in, please? I tell him."

I stepped inside. Everything looked exactly as I remembered it.

She went away and returned shortly. "He comes in a minute." Politely she showed me into the living room. "You sit, please."

"Thank you." I sat down on my sofa to wait.

Harry appeared. He looked fitter and younger than I remembered. In a not-unfriendly tone, he said, "Well, now, what's this about?"

"I have a proposal," I said, crisply.

He smiled. "Not a penny more. The agreement's signed, sealed and delivered. It's airtight."

I said, with dignity, "I came about a job."

"Job?"

"Housekeeper. I'll clean, cook, serve your meals, do your laundry, sew on your buttons. For wages."

The young woman had crept into the room, and sat listening.

"A business arrangement. As you know, I've had years of experience, I'm well qualified."

"You're insane," he said, genially. He stood up and danced a sailor's hornpipe, then sat down again and folded his arms. "Certifiably mad."

The young woman put a hand to her lips, looking worried.

"She'll be the mistress, I'll be the maid," I explained.

He rose, laughing. "Get out."

"No—don't," the young woman suddenly cried, though to whom wasn't clear. "You would like a cup of tea?" she asked me, anxiously. "It will take one minute only."

"Tea would be nice," I agreed.

While we waited, Harry examined his nails. Tea was brought in a twinkling. In polite silence, the three of us sipped, as though in some formal religious ceremony.

I put down my cup and rose to leave. "Please think it over. I'll call tomorrow to get your answer."

Harry stayed seated, staring into space. The young woman saw me to the door.

As I left, I was struck by the beauty of the pale pink vetch growing profusely in front of the house. "I planted this. May I take just a little?"

"*Nein!*" Her face grew distorted with rage. "No flowers!" she screamed. "Go! Go!" She slammed the door shut.

I awoke, weeping, with "Go! Go!" still ringing in my head.

# 4

WITH THE MIDDLE OF JUNE, warm weather arrived. And so did he.

"Iris? I'm Leo Tanner."

I looked up from the ironing board. What had I expected? Not those dark slanted eyes that looked almost Oriental, not that hawk nose sharply dividing his face. Yet there was something almost dapper about him in that pinstriped suit.

"Welcome aboard," he said, and held out his hand. We shook, formally. In that moment I felt the dynamic of the household change in some fashion.

"Do you have what you need? Are you comfortably settled?" Those eyes took my measure. A strange feeling, to be X-rayed thus. Woe betide any adversary, I thought, in court or out.

"Her desk could use some first aid, darling." Paula had followed him in, carrying groceries. "The little spinet."

"Tomorrow, first thing." He loosened his tie. "I'm going up to change. If anyone calls, say I haven't yet arrived, take a message." He left, whistling *The March of the Toreadors*.

Paula moved about, unpacking the groceries. "We bought lobster. Leo will cook tonight. We'll probably eat outside."

And where should I be while they ate? Hovering to serve? Or should I make myself scarce to give them privacy?

She answered my thought. "We won't need you for dinner, but I'd like you to clear up afterwards." Now her glance took in the ironing. "Good, you've done my linen skirt." Her voice was warmer than I had ever heard it. She took the skirt and a blouse and some lingerie and left. I heard her almost running up the stairs.

No doubt about it, she was different when he was there; she laughed more, talked more, all in a somewhat higher register. The tempo of life in the house changed, too: the telephone began to ring, people called with invitations to lunch, dinner, tennis, sailing. Because more people had arrived? Or was it simply that *he* was here?

He stayed through Monday, that first weekend. In the mornings he swam before breakfast; after breakfast he spent time in his study. While he worked, she would swim her daily thirty laps, make calls, do errands.

The first morning he came into the kitchen as I was getting breakfast ready and asked if he might go to my rooms to see about my desk. "Anything else, while I'm there?"

"The bedroom window sticks."

"I'll check it."

In shorts and a faded polo shirt, the dapper quality had disappeared. An improvement. He looked—not younger, especially, but fit, vital, full of a restless energy that seemed held ready below the surface.

She came in and I served their breakfast.

"I'm going into town, Leo. Anything you need?"

"Just *The Times*. There may be something on the Delmonico deal. A reporter called yesterday after talking to George . . ."

She had told me briefly about the Delmonico deal. Leo was one of a group negotiating to buy a theater which the city had been threatening to raze. It was this that was keeping him in the city.

". . . George said more than he should have, considering nothing's signed. It could throw the entire project out of whack. Is there more coffee?"

"Iris, we'd like more coffee, please. How's Jerry getting along these days?"

"As usual. Still ignoring deadlines. He doesn't seem to realize Herman means it this time about pulling out."

"Oh, you'll bring Jerry around. You always do. You're awfully good at that."

Pride in her voice. Not just pride in him for the vicarious aura his success conferred on *her*, but, from the sound of it, a genuine appreciation of his ability.

Harry had once said to me angrily, "You don't seem to understand that I'm highly respected in my field."

He was wrong. I did understand, of course I did. What else were all those publications about, all the conferences here and abroad, all the meetings at which he was key speaker? Not to mention his income. But I counted all that as unimportant against the fact that he was a cold and bloodless individual. Oh, he could be charming, yes, whenever he felt like it, but his charm was a calculated commodity, produced at professional functions, say, or when we entertained or were entertained by colleagues, or when we went to visit Callie at school. Not for me, never for me. So far as I could tell, he didn't especially summon it up to impress other women. In a way, I wish he had. We had been married quite a while before I came to the conclusion that he didn't much like women—the gender as a whole, that is. I don't mean there was anything ambiguous about his sexuality; he was hetero, all right, but he wasn't really comfortable with women.

"Iris—" Her voice crackled from the intercom while I was sweeping the kitchen. "—I forgot my terry robe. I think it's on the bed. Will you bring it to the pool, please?"

I went upstairs. There it was, lying on the bed which I hadn't yet made. The bed looked somewhat more rumpled than usual. For a second I pictured them together. For some reason I had been totally without sexual desire ever since Oliver. Yesterday I had felt the smallest twitch, the merest reflex, on meeting Leo. But it meant nothing, was illusory as the feeling of warmth or cold in an amputated limb. Sex held no more interest for me these days than a flight into space. I felt no envy now as I looked at that bed, only a vague curiosity: What kind of lover was he? How did she respond? How often did they make love?

I took the robe to the pool, and waited as she climbed out of the water. For a woman of her age, that was a damn good body—lean without being stringy, neat breasts, firm thighs. Slightly bowlegged—a minor flaw. The bright blue of the pool set off her blondeness and tan as she wrapped herself in the robe and shook out her hair.

"Mrs. Lassiter called. She'd like you to call her back before eleven," I said.

"Thank you. By the way, you might bring a broom down here and sweep off the flagstones."

We walked back to the house together.

"Is that new?" Her tone was suddenly less distant.

"Is what—?"

"That shirt. It suits you."

It was a cotton peasant shirt I'd acquired on a long-ago trip with Harry to Brazil. "Not new. Falling apart, it's been laundered so often."

"Attractive." Suddenly, she spoke in a rush. "I adore pretty clothes, don't you?"

Hardly a statement of import, but this was the first spontaneous remark she had addressed to me, as one person to another. "Yes, I do."

"That's the first time I've seen you really smile, Iris. You tend to put on a long face, you know."

Oh? Would she be smiling if our situations were reversed?

The way I felt must have showed, for she said quickly, "Oh, dear, have I offended you? I didn't mean—" Her hands fluttered, she gave an uncertain little laugh and hurried on ahead.

While I was sweeping the flagstones around the pool, Leo Tanner suddenly materialized. "The desk is fixed. So's the window. Do you use the desk much?"

"Quite a bit, to write letters. Notes from Underground, as it were." It slipped out without my thinking, like cocktail party repartee. Never mind. He'd seen me for what I was the moment we met—whatever, whoever, not a cipher. For her that might be a source of discomfort. For him I knew it presented no difficulty.

He smiled. "You should have a proper desk lamp, then. I'll see about it."

I watched him go. Something about him reminded me of Oliver. What was it? There was certainly no physical resemblance. Oliver had been rangy, with a brooding, faraway look. Then it came to me: Like Oliver, some quality in this man's glance, voice, the way he carried himself, showed that he enjoyed the company of women, was at ease with them, aware of them in all their facets. An awareness that was bound to evoke a like response.

Back at the house, she had turned on music; *Serenade for Strings* sounded joyfully through the rooms. She was humming as she came into the kitchen. Our little contretemps seemed to have been forgotten. "Well, I'm off. Leo's still on the phone. When he's through, tell him we're playing doubles with the Lassiters at three."

I watched through the window as she went out to the car. Even her walk was different—lighter, quicker, the walk of a younger woman. Was it possible that here in this antiseptic setting, I'd stumbled upon that rare phenomenon, a happy marriage?

On Sunday I was beginning to prepare their lunch when she came in looking sleek in white pants and striped T.

"Sorry, Iris, I forgot to say we won't need lunch, we're going sailing with the Benjamins. How does the rest of your day look?"

What did she mean, how did it look? I was supposed to be free after one o'clock Sundays. "I thought I'd go for a drive this afternoon."

She touched a hand to her hair. "I won't actually need you this afternoon, but I'd rather you stayed around today. The Benjamins might come back for dinner."

"But I thought Sundays—"

"Yes, but with summer upon us, we'll take each weekend as it comes. You can take off during the week instead."

This annoyed me. Apart from the fact that she was reneging on our arrangement, this meant I'd never know in advance when I'd be free; I'd never be able to make plans of my own for a specific occasion.

"Why don't you swim in the pool or sun on the beach down here? It's a perfect day for it."

True, but that wasn't the point. Dare I protest?

What difference did it make, though, at this stage? I had no special arrangements to cancel; no friends were waiting for me to join them. If ever I acquired a life of my own, my free time would be worth fighting for. Until then, it hardly mattered.

Lying on the beach later in my swimsuit, all visible parts of me oiled, I surveyed the prospect around me. Although the season hadn't officially started, there were quite a few people. Surely there must be some way to strike up an acquaintance? Perhaps if I sat up, I'd appear more accessible. I sat, glancing around hopefully, but no one approached to exchange amenities. No one even glanced in my direction. Should I move closer to someone? My chances would probably be better with a single or group than a twosome. That man and woman over there wouldn't do, absorbed in their books, enclosed in their couplehood. Nor would that trio of young people in their twenties. But over there, that rather sympatico-looking woman on her own on the yellow beach towel—?

Over the next hour, I picked up my blanket and moved my location several times, as though following the sun, settling down in propinquity to what seemed a likely prospect. But no one paid me any attention.

Finally I gave up and lay down again, feeling rejected, dejected. For a while I lay there listening wistfully to the distant murmur of voices, an occasional laugh, a shriek now and then from a child daring the frigid water. Then the warmth of the sun put me to sleep. As I slept, I seemed to hear the ocean's roar in the distance, as it roars when you put a shell to your ear. I seemed to hear the sound of waves breaking, then the drawing, sucking sound as the water pulled back. A voice spoke. I couldn't make out the words, but something—a fly? gnat?—touched my arm. I raised a hand to brush it away, but the touch was insistent, grew firmer, finally took my arm and shook it. The voice grew louder: *"Wake up!"*

With a shock, I awoke to find water lapping at my toes, and someone bending over me.

"You're alive, anyway!" He sounded relieved. "I'd begun to wonder. The tide's coming in. I thought you might float out to sea. Everyone's gone."

I sat up abruptly. It was true. The strip of beach still uncovered by water was devoid of people. The sun was considerably further along the sky. I looked at my watch. Five forty-five! I'd done nothing about dinner! Now I scrambled to my feet. "Thank you, I'm very grateful . . ." Hastily I gathered up my things. In my hurry, I dropped my book.

He retrieved it, glanced at it as he handed it back. "Good old *Ebenezer*. I keep recommending this in my store."

His store? A bookstore? It seemed to fit this plump, pink person with pale eyelashes, scanty hair, cord shorts that were a little too long, white shirt-tails flapping in the breeze.

*3 5*

He fumbled in his pocket and brought out a card. *Baxter's New and Used Books. Special Orders. Collections.* "I'm Graham Baxter."

"I'm Iris Prue."

"Are you here on vacation?"

"No, I work for some people who have a summer place here. Do you live here?"

"I live over the store in Merriam, ten miles down the road." He had come to see a collection of early Sherlockiana that someone who lived here was selling. "Out of my price range, unfortunately." Afterwards, strolling down to look at the sea, he'd come upon me lying there. "Like washed-up flotsam."

Washed-up. Never a truer word. "Thank you again. I must dash."

"Drop by the store, if you're down that way. I welcome browsers."

I had just stepped out of a fast shower when the telephone rang.

"Tanner residence."

"Who is this?" Her tone was impatient.

I bristled. What kind of game was she playing? "It's me," I announced tersely and ungrammatically.

"Who?"

Only then did I realize it wasn't Paula. "Iris Prue. The housekeeper."

"This is Beth Tanner. Is my mother there?"

She didn't sound like her mother now, it was only at first. Like Callie and me . . . We'd been constantly mistaken for each other over the phone; it was the only respect in which we resembled each other, I thought. "No, she—"

"My father, then?"

"They've gone sailing. Any message?"

"Never mind." She sounded disgruntled. "I'll call back this evening, maybe."

• • •

The Benjamins and another couple came back for dinner. "We'll eat outside, Iris. No rush—we're going to sit and have drinks for a while. I'll let you know when we're ready."

"Your daughter called."

She turned, quickly. "Did she leave a number?"

"She said she might call back this evening."

"That's all she said?"

"That's all."

While everyone sat on the deck with drinks, I prepared dinner. The sound of their voices drifting in as I worked made me feel more outcast than ever. It was always like this when guests were here; convivial occasions underscored my role as Cinderella. I banged a skillet down on the stove, not caring whether anyone heard. Let her hear! Let her hear and come in and—

It was Leo who appeared, however. "Is there more tonic?"

"Down there."

He lingered to watch as I stirred shrimp into rice. "What do you call that?"

"The Houdini Special. Stretches like magic to feed an infinite number." My voice was tart. Who cared?

Paula entered in a rush. "Darling, Martin's waiting for his refill! Iris, what's taking so long? It'll soon be too chilly to eat outdoors."

"You were supposed to let me know—"

But she had already hurried out again. "Well, you poor starving creatures," I heard her call, "I've got things back on the track! Dinner's almost ready!"

God, I was tired of being put in the wrong, tired of being unable to defend myself. How much longer could I stand it?

Everything was ready. I went out to the deck. "Dinner is served, in a manner of speaking."

Conversation stopped. With every eye fixed on me, I made a smart left turn and went back to the kitchen.

• • •

The guests left at ten-thirty. She came into the kitchen while I was still cleaning up. I braced myself. If she gave me a hard time, I'd—what? Hurl a saucepan? Tell her off? Quit?

"That was a very good dinner, Iris. Don't bother to finish this now. Leave it till morning."

A large concession, from her. Without a word I dried my hands and escaped upstairs, where I sat by my window staring out. How quiet it was. Here and there lights glimmered from the houses set among the trees. A distant church clock struck the hour weightily. Eleven o'clock and all's well. Not for me.

*Joanna, you were right.* Self-abnegation was beginning to get to me. This was an occupational hazard that hadn't occurred to me in advance.

Martin Benjamin, garbed in requisite blazer and tan, had sidled up to me in the kitchen after dinner. "What's someone like you doing in a job like this?" he'd inquired, silkily. Variant on a well-known theme. Too bad I was over the hill for that line of work. "Earning a living." I ran water noisily into the pot to soak the silverware.

"Where did you come from?"

"Out of the everywhere, into the here," I informed him, snappily, and made my exit, bearing garbage.

At midnight I undressed and got into bed. Lying there, I seemed to hear Callie, the way her voice filled with dismay whenever I called. Sharper than a serpent's tooth was right; I might as well ask a stone for help as ask my daughter.

Sleep was impossible. I got up, put on a windbreaker, and tiptoed downstairs through the darkened house and out to the deck. There I sat, regarding a low honey-colored moon that resembled a peach ripe for plucking.

Gradually I became aware of voices which seemed to be coming from the branches of the spruce overhead. It took me a moment to realize they were coming from the window directly above me. Their bedroom window.

"Beth didn't call back. I wonder what she wanted?"

"What she always wants, of course. A handout."

"You're so hard on her, Leo."

"What else does she usually want when she calls?"

"Why shouldn't we carry her for a while? At least until she's finished her studies."

"What studies? You mean dance lessons? You know as well as I do, Paula, you don't begin as a dancer at the age of twenty-nine."

"She's trying her best, Leo."

"No, she's just drifting. She gets by on money you slip her and your charge accounts. We're no help, letting her get away with this kind of existence."

"Leo, I wish—"

"I don't want to discuss it now, Paula. It's late. Let's get some sleep."

Long after silence had fallen, I still sat there, thinking. Thinking mainly about Callie, imagining a conversation she might have about me with a friend or lover. "She's just drifting," I could hear her say. "Always calling for a handout."

Next day I was out on the deck, washing down the outdoor furniture, when I heard her call from the deck outside their bedroom. "Darling!" That silvery voice floated over the landscape. "It's twelve o'clock! We're due at the Werners soon."

"I'd like to get this done first, Paula."

"I said we'd be prompt."

"Just ten more minutes."

"But, darling—"

Darling. Was it always thus, I wondered. Or—it suddenly occurred to me—was this specifically for my benefit? A labeling of territory, as it were.

"—can't you finish later?"

"Paula—" He stopped. "All right, I'll be in shortly."

Moments later he came into view, rubbing his palms together to brush off dirt. "Iris, would you leave that and come
here, please?"

I followed him to the garden.

"Would you mind finishing this for me? Clean it out around
the impatiens? I know this isn't within your bailiwick—"

"That's all right, I like gardening." I knelt on the grass.
"Do you want these incipient violets out?"

"Please." He lingered to watch. "You've done this kind
of thing before, I see."

"Yes. I used to have a garden."

Did my garden still exist, I wondered. Did Swiss Miss take
care of it?

"What kind of work did you do before you came here?"

"Kept house, mostly. My own. And took care of my family."
I tugged carefully at a recalcitrant root.

"You have children?"

"A daughter." It yielded at last, came cleanly away from
the clinging soil.

"Where?"

"San Francisco. Practicing law."

"Who's she with?"

"Phillips Reiner."

"Really? You must be proud of her." His voice held just
the shade of something. Surprised, I glanced up and caught
him looking somber.

"Leo, *please!*"

"Yes, Paula, I'm coming." Off he went.

The sun was at its zenith now. Perspiration dampened the
back of my neck as I worked. I sat back on my heels and
pushed my hair away from my face with the back of a dirt-
smeared hand. From here I could look down through the
trees to the heavy shapes of the rocks on the beach and the
ocean glittering beyond. Far out on the sea was a single
sailboat, looking toylike as it skittered along the sunstruck
water. Oliver, wherever you are, whatever you're doing, do
you ever think of me?

# 5

THE FIRST DAY OF SUMMER lay behind us. The local press reminded native residents to be patient with the influx of visitors. Jaguars, Mercedes, and Ferraris had added their exotic presence to the traffic proceeding slowly down High Street. Captain Bligh had taken on two helpers. All the motels, cottages, and summer homes were now occupied. Guests sat in the wicker chairs along the expansive porch of the huge old Staunton Inn fronting the harbor. Nowadays, I often took my lunch to the beach to eat in peace. Seated on the rocks, I'd watch herring gulls soar against the cerulean sky while sanderlings stepped fast and dainty at the water's edge.

Paula seemed dejected lately. Because of Beth? Beth had called a number of times recently. Through the closed door of the den, I'd heard Paula's voice reproving, pleading, though I couldn't make out the words.

Or was Paula upset about the fact that Leo was still turning up only infrequently?

"Now the work's finished, I think I'll come back for a while and keep you company," I'd heard her say, the last time he was in.

"What for? New York's like an oven. Everyone's gone. Stay put. I'll come when I can."

I could see why she'd made the offer. She was the one who needed company. Unmistakably she was left to her own devices when he wasn't there.

• • •

On June twenty-second my own mood was somewhat dark. It was my birthday, a time inevitably for taking stock. Taking stock, I found the outlook bleak.

I carried her lunch out to the deck, where she was reclining in shorts and halter, reading *The Times*.

She lowered the paper and took the tray. "Have you eaten yet?"

"No."

"Why don't you eat out here, then? It's far too nice to eat indoors."

Eat with her, did she mean? She must indeed be desperate for company if she was willing to risk our breaking bread together.

At first, we ate without speaking. If she wanted to chat, she would have to take the lead; I wasn't going to risk being snubbed.

Finally she broke the silence. "I went to Annabelle's but they're still out of the colors I want."

"Doesn't anyone else carry them?"

"Not here. I'll have to ask Leo to bring what I need when he comes."

My turn. "Care for cheese?" I passed it.

"This isn't the kind we had last week."

"No, this is Morbier. At the peak, I think."

"Yes, it's really quite good."

Oh dear, hard work. I kept wishing I were down on the rocks, with a sandwich.

"Did you see this?" She held out the newspaper. *Saving the Delmonico* read the headline. *Saying no to the bulldozers may also mean saying no to stockholders.* There was a lengthy story, and a picture of Leo with two others described as "key figures." "When I see the vast amount involved, it makes me nervous. But Leo says life isn't worth living if you don't take risks. He knows what he's doing, of course—"

The ring of the telephone cut her off. Paula reached for

it. "Hello? Yes, it is. Who? Just a minute. Iris, it's for you."
She sounded faintly surprised. "Take it in my study, if you
like."

Wondering, I went in and closed the door behind me.

"Felicitations! Many happy returns!"

"Joanna!" It was the first time we'd spoken since I'd left
Boston. "Wonderful to hear you!" At the same time it gave
me a pang, reminding me how much I missed talk, friendship.

"How's everything going?" she asked.

I told her I was settled in, getting used to everything. "Just
now, we're having a cosy lunch together, the Mistress and
I. How are things with you?"

Not much to report, she said. Hilary was interning at the
Peabody. Walt had a summer job in construction. Nat had
torn a ligament playing tennis. "I'm in the throes of learning
Greek—" She stopped abruptly.

"Why Greek?"

"Oh well, we're going to Greece next month. It'll be
horribly hot and crowded, I'm not really that keen, but it's
the only time Nat can get away . . ."

She made a vacation in Greece sound like a drag—who
in her right mind would want it? I understood. You don't
discuss your four-star dinner with someone who's on bread
and water. Don't worry, Joanna, it's not travel I yearn for
right now.

"Iris, listen." Her voice changed. "Callie called."

"Called *you?*"

"She could hardly call *you*—she didn't know where you
were. Why didn't you tell her?"

"She hasn't exactly given signs of caring."

"Don't be silly, of course she cares!"

Did she? Every time I thought of that last call I'd made
to Callie, I felt sick . . .

Midnight, it had been, an hour when small grinning creatures came and sat on my shoulder and I could almost hear

my teeth chatter. Nine o'clock out there on the Coast. Please, let her be home.

She was.

"Callie, listen, I hate to ask, but I'm really in rather urgent need . . ." I kept calm and explained it all sensibly, I thought. "So if you could lend me, say, five hundred dollars—"

"But, Mother—" My heart sank at that expostulatory tone— "you simply can't go on like this! You must find some work or get some training or—"

"I'm trying, but meanwhile I have to live, Callie. If you could possibly—"

"I don't have it. I've just moved into a new apartment and—"

"Tell your father you need some money."

Silence.

"Are you suggesting I ask Daddy for money as though it's for myself, but actually to give to you?" She sounded incredulous, and also disgusted.

"Not give. A loan. Tell him you need it for furniture or something. You know he'll give you whatever you ask for."

I couldn't help the bitterness that crept into my voice. Harry had always showered Callie with largesse. As a child, an adolescent, a college student, Callie had only to ask in order to receive. When I'd pointed out this was not the best thing, Harry had said grimly, "My daughter is not going to have to struggle."

Surprisingly, Callie had suddenly turned independent two years ago. She had allowed Harry to pay for law school (from which she had graduated *summa cum laude*, editor of the review), but she had announced that she intended to take care of herself entirely after that. She seemed to be making good on this.

"Callie, I'm in real trouble."

"You wouldn't be, if you hadn't—"

"I'm not the first woman in history to have gotten a divorce, Callie!"

4 4

"I don't mean that!" She sounded angry now. "I mean the way you humiliated Daddy! You didn't care about anything, you didn't think twice, just ran off with your—your—that man half your age!"

I couldn't help wondering how I had managed to produce a daughter like Callie. She was fair, delicate-looking, with skin that seemed almost translucent. But inside she was tough. She would probably be a first-rate lawyer. Heaven help the poor wretches who opposed her in court.

"For the record, Callie, Oliver was exactly six years younger than me." Was. As though he had shackled off these mortal coils. "Anyway, that's hardly relevant, is it? At this stage?"

"Look, I can send you two hundred dollars, but that's all I can manage! Get some therapy or something! I can't deal with this!"

The line went dead. I thought at first we'd been cut off. Then I realized.

Would it have been any different if I hadn't left Harry for someone else, but simply left him? I had once asked Callie that when she had come to see me soon after I moved in with Oliver. She was still in law school then. She had come to ask me to go back to Harry.

I said, amazed, "Did he send you?"

"Certainly not. I'm capable of thinking for myself."

She had stood all the while, refusing to sit down. "Not here," she'd said, as though in a house of plague. How young she had seemed, and vulnerable, her straight hair falling past her shoulders. I'd wanted to put my arms around her and reassure her, "Don't worry, everything will be all right." Still wrapped in my own happiness with Oliver, I had truly believed it. Everything would work out; Harry's anger, which didn't bother me, and Callie's hurt, which did, would gradually dissolve, all this *sturm und drang* would subside and I could begin my new life free and clear.

She said, grudgingly, "He misses you."

Missed me? Harry? Harry hadn't cared about me for years.

All Harry cared about was that another man had been in the picture—an affront to his pride.

"I should have known! A painter! Artsy! You'll be sorry!" He had shaken his fist.

His anger had seemed to make things easier, somehow. But not for long.

After that phone call, Callie had sent the promised check, but with it had come a cool note advising me to learn to stand on my own two feet, get credentials, get a job, get counselling, get organized. Get lost, kiddo, I'd thought, and had sent an equally cool note of thanks for the money.

I recounted this to Joanna now. "After that kind of letter, I wasn't about to tell her my plans. She already views me as an embarrassment. Heaven forbid I should bother her further." My voice was heavy with sarcasm. But inwardly I suddenly felt confused. Why did I keep feeling I had to prove myself to Callie, of all people?

"Iris, try to understand—it hasn't been easy on Callie either, all this."

"All what?"

"The break-up with Harry. You and Oliver. Your problems after he left. And—dealing with a father who still wants to own her as though she's a child. I suspect he's used the divorce as a further excuse to try to keep her under his thumb. As in 'now that your mother's skipped off, you and I must stick together.' "

"They should. They deserve each other, a pair of cold—"

"Stop it! You know better than that! Let me tell you—" her voice grew heated—"you aren't the easiest person to deal with, either! I can sometimes see why Callie keeps her distance!" It sounded as though she were breathing heavily.

I gave her a second to calm down. "Did you tell her?"

"Tell her what?"

"Where I am. What I'm doing."

"Yes. Isn't that all right?"

"It makes not the slightest difference to me one way or the other. Er—what did she say?"

"Not much. I think she was . . . taken aback. Which is understandable."

"I suppose." Suddenly I felt despairing. "Joanna, I don't know, some days I can't see where I am, where I'm going—"

"Iris, listen, come back to Boston, to some kind of normal life."

"Doing what?"

"You could always clerk at Filene's till you line up something better."

"Who wants to clerk at Filene's?"

"Who wants to do what *you're* doing, for heaven's sake? You don't make sense! Bizarre, Callie calls it, and she's right! 'Why can't my mother be like other women who get divorced?' Callie said. 'Other women find appropriate jobs, they cope.' "

There was something wrong with me, she meant. Was it true? Did I lack the kind of fundamental core which enabled people to deal with problems, the world, life? Was some vitally necessary element missing, the fact not immediately apparent because on the surface I looked normal? A chasm seemed to open before me. I stared, terrified, into the depths. Perhaps anyone with an eye to see could tell that I was only bluffing, that in reality I was like one of those old Western movie sets, a facade of shops and saloons with nothing at all behind it.

Enough. I dismissed the image forthwith. Joanna—and no doubt even Callie, too—meant no harm, but this kind of talk certainly didn't help anything.

"Joanna, it may seem absurd to Callie, to you, but this job seems to be all I can handle at present. What I could really use from Callie—or anyone—is a few encouraging words, rather than disparagement."

"Iris—"

"It's no bed of roses here. I'm lonely, too. But it probably isn't a bad thing to be in a totally different setting, away from people and places I know. In a way, it wipes the slate clean. A fresh start."

"Iris, that's not starting. It's putting off starting."

"Whatever, I can't leave here. No matter how much Callie disapproves," I added, bitterly.

"Disapproves? That's not—" She broke off. "Callie may be your daughter, but you don't seem to understand her one whit. It's not a matter of disapproving. She's scared."

"Of what?"

"Of your behavior, that's what. You're acting as though you've gone to pieces."

"Gone to pieces?" My tone was icy.

"She's sees you're not seriously trying—"

"Not *trying?* What in heaven's name does she think I'm doing here?" It was difficult to keep my voice below a shout. "Does she think I'm having fun? Does she think I'm enjoying it? Scared? Yes, she's scared her upscale friends will find out—"

"Okay, Iris, that's it, enough!" I heard her let out her breath. "Guess I'll mind my own business from now on. But listen, we're leaving in two weeks, back August twenty-fifth. Meanwhile, call whenever. Stay in touch. Promise?"

"Don't worry, Joanna. I'm quite all right."

"Promise," she insisted.

Dear Joanna, my friend despite everything, my tie to the outer world—a world that seemed to slip further away with each day that passed.

"I promise."

An hour later, Paula was seated at the kitchen table, making one of her lists, while I stood on top of the stepstool to take from the cabinet's highest shelf some goblets she wanted washed.

Just then, the doorbell rang.

I hesitated, clutching glasses gingerly in one hand while holding on to the cabinet with the other, trying to decide whether to descend with the glasses or leave them.

Paula looked up. "All right, Iris, stay where you are, I'll get the door."

In a moment she was back.

"Iris—"

I put the last of the glasses safely on the counter, stepped down, and turned to see her holding a florist's box.

"For you." Her tone was carefully uninterested.

"Oh. Thank you." I took it, wondering, wishing she weren't around—I'd have preferred to open this in private. Perhaps she guessed, for she left and went upstairs.

I opened the box. Inside lay roses the colour of clotted cream. I read the card: *Happy birthday. Best wishes. Callie.*

My pleasure was mixed with disappointment. She should have called. This was a cop-out, kept distance between us. *Best wishes.* How loving, how fond. Still, at least she had thought of me, had remembered.

Paula returned as I was arranging the roses in a vase.

"How lovely." She hesitated. "What's the occasion—may I ask?"

"My daughter sent them. For my birthday."

"Your birthday's today?" She seemed nonplussed. "Well— happy birthday!"

"Thank you."

She stood watching. "Have you any special plans this evening?"

Oh, I thought I'd hop on a plane to Paris. Actually, friends are throwing a bash for me at the club.

"I might go to the movies. There's a Judy Garland film at the Regent."

"Well—would you like company?" She sounded tentative.

Oh, dear. What could I say? Ah, well, it would be a change, anyway, from being alone. "Why not?" It sounded less than

4 9

welcoming. I tried again. "That would be nice." Weak. The best I could manage, however.

"Good. Would you like to go out to dinner afterwards, to celebrate?"

Caught off guard, I didn't know how to respond. I would certainly enjoy going to dinner at a decent restaurant. But would we be two women out for the evening, or would her role be that of Lady Bountiful while I played the grateful retainer? Still, what else would I have done this evening? Sat alone in the stuffy darkness of the Regent? Eaten clams by myself afterwards at The Crow's Nest, noted for its pervasive smell of deep-fat frying?

"Thank you. That sounds very pleasant."

She looked pleased. "I'll call the club and book a table."

It felt like a time warp, to be sitting at dinner in this kind of place, with no thought of the cost. Through the wall of glass, the moon shone down on the boats bobbing as they rode at anchor. At four-second intervals, the long beam from the Wixsey Light swung across the water.

"They do a good Crab Louis here. Rack of lamb is good, too. What else would you recommend, Simon?"

With flourishes, Simon imparted his wisdom. The wine waiter offered suggestions. Dinner was brought, wine was poured, the waiters retired to a discreet distance.

She raised her glass. "Cheers." A real smile, for once. "May future birthdays bring—" The smile wavered as she strove for an appropriate sentiment—"whatever you wish for."

What I wished for. To be gone from here ultimately. Or rather, to have the means and strength to be gone. "Thank you. It's kind of you to do this. I'm enjoying it."

"Good. So am I."

For a while, we chatted about Judy Garland movies, and then about other young musical stars from the past.

"Do you remember Deanna Durbin? And Shirley Temple? No, you're not old enough . . ."

I had seen a couple of Shirley Temple movies on television, I said.

"When I was a child, I absolutely *lived* for Shirley Temple movies . . ." Enthusiasm warmed her voice. She leaned forward, smiling. "I used to cut her pictures out of movie magazines and stick them in a scrapbook. I tried tap-dancing up and down the stairs, like Shirley and Bojangles."

I smiled. Something about that image appealed to me, evoking childhood memories of my own, though my own ambitions had encompassed tutus and ballet shoes tied with satin ribbons. Moira Shearer, in *The Red Shoes,* had danced through all my childish dreams. "Yes. Dancing class on Saturday mornings—"

"Not for me." Her voice was suddenly dry. "We had no money for lessons, though my father gave me tapshoes for my seventh birthday. Anyway, there wasn't anyone giving dancing lessons where I grew up."

"Where was that?"

"A tiny place you've never heard of, in northern Michigan." She sipped her wine. "Tell me more about your daughter. What kind of law is she in?"

"Litigation."

"Is she married?"

"No." Come to think of it, could I be sure? She told me nothing about herself, held herself away as though I were an illness that might infect her.

"Do you visit?"

"I haven't had the money to travel." Nor, for that matter, an invitation.

Her next words took my breath away. "Does she like you?"

"*Like* me?" How dare she! On the other hand, I was astounded at the perceptiveness her words seemed to show.

"I'm sorry." Her cheeks were faintly pink. "I didn't mean—"

51

"It's all right. Just that—I'm not sure I really know the answer." I considered. "She used to, I think. But not any more."

"No?" Her fingers smoothed the peach damask. "She sent roses. Beth hasn't acknowledged my birthday for years with so much as a card."

Why was she telling me this? Was it the wine? Or simply that she, too, needed someone to talk to?

But now, as though realizing, she sidestepped into safer territory. There was some kind of fungus on the tall spruce, Dr. Yarker wasn't sure he could save it. She was thinking of changing the living room around, moving the piano to the far end; would it be an improvement? I said I thought so. A new gallery had opened in Benbow; would I like to go along some time and help choose something for the front hall? I said I would.

Silence fell. A couple passed, and the woman said, brightly, "Paula, how are you?" then went ahead without waiting for an answer. Paula hardly seemed to notice.

"Iris, there's something I've been meaning to ask. What does your husband do? Ex-husband, I mean."

"He's a plastic surgeon." Surgeon made of plastic? More like heavy metal.

"He must do well then, financially. I'd have thought alimony—"

"But I wanted a divorce quickly, so I didn't hold out for what I should have had."

"You don't have family who can help?"

"My parents died soon after I was married, in an accident. My father was a teacher. There wasn't much money. The little there was, I spent years ago. I was married, I didn't foresee—" Crazy, crazy, crazy! I didn't want to think about it, couldn't bear to be reminded of my foolish mistakes. Quick, change the subject. "How long have you lived in New York?"

She had gone there right out of high school, she said,

hoping to model. They said she wasn't tall enough to model fashion, but her face photographed well and she'd modeled cosmetics, jewelry, hats. "I got to know lots of people, went to lots of parties. Someone invited me to a cast party after a show. That's where I met Leo . . ."

In the adjoining room, someone began to play cocktail piano. *How much do I love you, I'll tell you no lie, How deep is the ocean, How high is the sky* . . . Behind Paula, that long, luminous shaft of light flared through the darkness, swung away, returned. "You're watching the Light?" She turned to look. "It's a pretty spot out there on the headland. Have you been there?"

"No."

"Back in the days when the lights were operated by hand, the keepers' wives kept the lights going for their men if they fell ill or went off to get supplies, or to rescue someone from a shipwreck. A lonely life that must have been, for those women . . ." She sipped her coffee, then put the cup down, fitting it precisely into the saucer. "I can change a lightbulb— that's about all. Still, I'm not complaining. I'm really very fortunate. My marriage is everything I ever hoped for."

She spoke with an earnestness that was somehow touching, that last not a boast but grateful acknowledgement. All at once, she seemed unguarded, genuine, human.

# 6

THERE IS A BIRD —is it the housefinch?—that jumps one step forward, one step back, as it pecks at seed. Paula was like that. After that birthday dinner, things seemed to improve between us; some barrier had been lowered, some progress made. Not that we exchanged further confidences, nor did we turn into bosom friends. Still, she talked to me more now, and addressed me with reasonable civility. Quite often we ate meals together. When she went into town to do errands, she made it a point to ask whether I needed anything—for myself, not just for the house—and if there were, she would pick it up for me, shampoo or stamps or whatever.

Once she brought me a book I'd ordered. As I gave her the money for it, she said, "Should you be buying this sort of thing?"

The jacket cover was luridly misleading, and I thought she meant she disapproved of my taste, but that wasn't it.

"You're not that flush. Why spend money on books you can get free from the library?"

I said, annoyed, "That's my business, I believe."

She looked disconcerted. "All I meant was, you're not very practical, for someone on a budget."

She sounded like Joanna. I suddenly regretted my tone, though not my words. "I'm sorry. I didn't mean to be rude."

"And I didn't mean to interfere. But I must say, Iris—"

she shook her head—"you seem to work against your own best interests at times."

Together, we went to the gallery in Benbow. It turned out to be a different, and quite pleasant, afternoon. She favoured a hard-edge abstract, white and ice-blue, *Polar Masses*. I was inclined to a busy Matisse-like work called *Hijinks*, with lots of pattern and color, though naturally I didn't press my opinion.

To my surprise, she said finally, "Let's take them both home and see."

We did. After lengthy consideration of each in turn, she pronounced her verdict, stepping back from where *Hijinks* hung on the long white wall. "Iris, you're right. This is definitely the one. I'm really very pleased."

There was no denying we had crossed some line. Which made all the more difficult the occasions when she reverted to Lady of the Manor.

One of those occasions came when I next asked to use the car on my day off. Normally that was Sunday, but this time I'd asked for Saturday instead. Leo again wasn't coming, so things would be quiet at the house. I couldn't see that my services would be required.

She agreed to Saturday. But when I asked to take the station wagon, she hesitated. "Do you really need it?"

"Yes. There's somewhere I specifically want to go."

"How far?"

"Just ten miles. To Merriam."

"It's been making an odd noise lately, haven't you noticed? I'd rather you used it only for essential errands, until Leo's had a look at it." She paused. "Anyway, I don't see why you have to keep tearing all over the place."

With an effort I kept my voice level. "How I use my own time is entirely my affair."

Her manner changed to one of injured dignity. "Naturally,

I didn't intend—Oh, by all means take it, if you feel you must. I only hope the long drive won't cause any damage."

Long drive? Damage? What was this about, exactly?

As I backed the wagon out of the garage that afternoon, a flash of movement drew my eyes to an upper window. I glanced up just in time to glimpse Paula watching, before she moved quickly out of sight.

Graham Baxter seemed genuinely pleased to see me.

"You found your way!" Smiling, he shook my hand. "I think you'll find where everything is. Used books through the arch there, paperbacks this way. If there's anything you can't find, ask me." Dressed in chinos, button-down shirt and a tie, he looked considerably more presentable than he had on the beach. "You don't have to rush off, I hope?"

"No, it's my day off. Business is booming, I see."

"Yes. I'm running a coupon offer. Makes me feel I'm selling groceries, but you have to do it."

He excused himself to attend to a customer and I went off to cruise the shelves. It was the kind of place where time goes by without your noticing. The shelves were well stocked and well organized. A coffeemaker stood on a low table between easy chairs. Strains of Mozart played softly in the background. Hanging ferns and Swedish ivy turned towards the encouraging light that came through the windows.

Half an hour passed, then an hour. I had settled down with a book of E. B. White and was quite content, but Graham kept coming over at intervals. "Roy will be down soon to keep an eye, then we'll go round the corner to Nowell's for a drink. That's our neighborhood pub. Jim Nowell and I play chess occasionally."

"Don't feel you have to entertain me. I'm quite content."

Around four o'clock the quiet was suddenly broken by the sound of footsteps clattering down unseen stairs, and a young man appeared. He had the kind of face seen on stone cherubs ornamenting fountains. Tight blonde curls formed a cap for his head. Above jeans that left no doubt of his gender, his T-shirt bore the sequined outline of a coiled snake, head raised, tongue flickering.

"Gimme the keys, Baxie, I'm taking off."

English, he sounded, though not fresh off the boat.

"Roy—"

"Come on, Baxie, be a sport! I'm going to see Pete. He knows a guy at Showplace, says he can get me something there for weekends maybe."

Graham sighed and handed something over.

"How about small change?" The voice turned wheedling. "Come on, mate!"

After a moment, Graham rang open the register. "But that's it for the week, you've already—"

"You're a prince, Baxie!" He flashed a grin, and was gone.

More customers came and Graham was kept busy. Then there was a lull. He came over. "I'm closing at six. Would you stay and have dinner with me upstairs?"

The apartment was tiny but charming. The glass in the windows was wavy with age. The floor was covered with a golden Bokhara. Delft tiles surrounded the fireplace, before which stood a jar filled with branches of white pine.

My offer of help with dinner was declined. "There isn't room, and anyway, I like to cook." He donned a denim apron.

He had had this place for two years, he said. Before that he had worked in various bookstores in New York, always dreaming of having a place of his own. He used to come here for vacations. Two elderly sisters had owned the shop then. "It was mostly a lending library, with a few bestsellers for sale. When Hattie died, Babe decided to retire. So here I am. It's wonderful when the season's over and the crowds go home, but business more or less comes to a halt. Fortunately my expenses are minimal. Roy gives me a hand, though I can't say books are really his interest. He's a musician." He nodded at the guitar that lay on the cushioned window seat.

"Please sit, dinner's ready." He placed a dish of scallops and mushrooms on the table. "Roy used to have a band of his own in England, called Serpent. They made an album a few years ago—*Slippery Love*. Not my kind of thing, I have to admit, but then, as Roy says, I'm an old fart, aren't I?" He smiled apologetically. "He came over here when his band split up, thought he'd get something to do over here, but he had bad luck, it didn't work out. He was going through a difficult time when I met him." He poured wine, tasted it, then filled our glasses. "When we came up here, I thought he'd be able to get local engagements, but there doesn't seem to be much available. Well, it's not easy for him. I like it here but he misses New York, excitement. Try the bread, I bake my own." He proffered the basket. "What brought you to this part of the world?"

"In ten words or less, I was divorced, broke, needed work."

"Housekeeping?" He eyed me. "Not exactly your cup of tea, I'd have thought."

"Nothing else came along."

"Nothing?"

"Nothing I seemed qualified for—at a salary I could live on."

"Housekeeping pays well, then?"

"No, but the fringes are good. It puts a better roof over my head than I could afford otherwise."

"How many in the house?"

"Just two, and he's not around much. There's a daughter, but she's only a voice on the telephone. What's in these heavenly scallops?"

At ten o'clock I got ready to leave. Graham came out to the car with me. The night air was clear and mild, the moon a slender, tipsy crescent.

As though coming to a decision, Graham spoke. "A few of us get together here in the shop to read plays once a month. Sundays, usually. Would you like to join us?"

"Would I!"

"You'll make an even half dozen. It's a congenial group. I think you'll enjoy it. We're doing *Pygmalion* next. July 12th, seven-thirty. Don't forget."

"Not bloody likely! Graham, thank you. For dinner, for everything!"

I put the key in the ignition and started the car. Or tried to. The motor turned over, stuttered politely, and died. I tried again. And again.

"Battery?"

"I don't think so."

"How's the gas?"

"Half a tank."

Remembering Paula's objections now, I felt distinctly uneasy. While I kept trying in vain to bring the engine to life, a car drove up, tires squealing.

Graham brightened. "Here's Roy! He'll know what to do. He's awfully good with mechanical things."

Roy got out and sauntered over, smoothing his curls with both hands. In the moonlight the sequins on his T-shirt glittered. "What's up?"

"I'm not sure."

"Move over, lemme take a crack at it."

He got behind the wheel and tried to start the motor. Nothing. He raised the hood and looked inside. We all looked.

"Beats me. Could be the choke. Or the fuel pump, maybe. Better call Bloor's."

My heart sank. We all trooped upstairs and Graham called the garage. Someone would be over in half an hour.

Roy opened the refrigerator. "What's to eat?"

"Scallops. Soup."

"I mean real food, man. Got any pizza? Here's some beer,

anyway." He sat down with the beer. "So what's the deal?" He gave me a look. "Where did you blow in from?"

"I'm sorry, I completely forgot! Iris, this is Roy. Roy, this is Iris Prue. We met on the beach, Roy."

"No kidding. Get you a beer, Irene?"

"Thanks, no."

He turned his head and the light was full on him. I realized then that though he was young, he wasn't quite the boy he'd seemed at first. Early thirties, anyway.

"While we're waiting, Roy, why don't you play something for Iris?" Graham sounded like a doting parent.

Roy took a swallow of beer, wiped his mouth and picked up the guitar. He played a few chords, tuned it, eased himself into a more comfortable position. "Here's something from my album. It's called 'Getting There.' "

I was prepared, for politeness' sake, to grit my teeth and appear enthusiastic; like Graham, I didn't much care for today's popular music. But a surprise awaited me. As soon as Roy began to play, an air of authority came over him. He cradled the instrument with confidence, his fingers moved with tender certainty across the strings. Playing, he was straight ahead, no tricks or gimmicks. He sang well, too; his voice wasn't phenomenal, but it didn't have the quasi whine that was currently fashionable. And his phrasing was good; he clearly had a sense of the words and sang them with meaning. *Getting there . . . It's gonna take time, but I'm getting there. It's gonna be tough, with no time for play, there's no easy way, but I'll get there . . . Believe me, I'll get there . . .*

Where would a Roy want to get, I wondered. What was his next step, from here? There would be a next step, that much was certain. Poor Graham, I thought, watching his face. Was it inevitable that, in love, there was always a taker and a giver? In the early years with Harry, I'd been the taker. With Oliver, I had learned the other role, with a vengeance. Oliver had taken everything from me—including, finally, himself. Graham, look out! Not that he needed me to tell him. He must have decided a long time ago that Roy was worth the risk.

With perfect timing, Roy remained still, bent over the instrument, as the last notes faded. Finally, he looked up.

I thanked him and told him I was impressed. "Did you write that?"

"Yeah. Damn good, right?" The wide, brash grin returned.

Just then, a horn tooted demandingly.

The mechanic said he thought it was the fuel pump. "Have to tow it. We'll test it tomorrow."

I tried not to think of Paula's reaction as I watched the car jolt away at the end of a chain.

"Come on, Iris, I'll drive you home."

"Don't bother, Baxie, I'll do it." Roy got behind the wheel. "All aboard, Irene!"

I felt vaguely uneasy. "Ride with us, Graham?"

"Nah, he's got things to do. I'm free as a bird." Roy laughed exuberantly, then gunned the motor. "Hop in."

There seemed no help for it. I got in.

Graham reached in and touched Roy's arm. "Take it easy, Roy."

"Ah, Baxie, lay off, will you? Okay, here we go!"

Away we roared. I fiddled urgently with the seat belt. "Doesn't this work?"

"The catch sticks sometimes." He reached down and it clicked into place. "Don't worry. I'll deliver you safe and sound. Never lost a fan yet."

Always a first time, I thought, averting my eyes from the road as we hurtled along.

"You really liked my song, right?"

"Yes." My voice was faint. Images of gory splatter filled my head.

"Haven't written much lately. Nothing to get the juices running up here in the boonies. Know what I mean?"

"*Watch out!*" I shrieked as we headed for an abutment.

Chortling, he veered over.

God in heaven, what had I gotten into?

"So you're a friend of Baxie's, huh? Poor old Baxie needs a friend, Christ knows. Sits around like a fucking old maid, goes nowhere, does nothing. I keep telling him he'd better get moving if he wants a little life. It goes fast, man!" He took a curve at such speed that I was thrown heavily against him. "Hey, keep your hands off, this is young meat here!" He pounded on the wheel, laughing crazily.

He was on something, of course. I should have realized. What had possessed me to get in this car with him? Thank heaven we were almost there.

Minutes later, we pulled up in the driveway.

He whistled. "Some pad! How about asking me in for a little refreshment? Or a smoke? I carry my own."

"I'm sorry, I can't. This isn't my house." I fumbled with trembling fingers to get the belt undone, but it wouldn't release.

"So what? Your friends won't mind."

"They're not my friends. I work here, I'm the housekeeper." Damn this thing!

"Is that right?" Suddenly he leaned forward, reached out a hand and squeezed my right breast, hard.

Furious, smarting with pain, I slapped his hand away, somehow wrenched the belt undone and jumped from the car. His laughter followed as I hurried, almost running, to the house. "See you, Irene!" The car took off, tires screeching.

The door swung inward just as I put the key in the lock. Paula loomed dimly out of the interior. "You're late!"

"You mean, there's a curfew?" My voice was acid, but I was too upset about Roy to care.

"I was beginning to worry in case of an accident." She seemed genuinely concerned, I now realized. "The car—"

Of course. The car, naturally. Oh dear, time to face the music.

"The car wouldn't start. I got a ride home."

Her expression became everything I'd dreaded. "What happened?" Her voice was steely.

I explained. We stood facing each other as though about to square off. It might happen, I thought, if she went on like this.

"You called the automobile club, I take it?"

For some reason, this hadn't occurred to me. "No, I'm afraid I—"

"Why not? There'll be towing charges."

"I'm sorry, I simply didn't think—"

"You *simply don't think* about a good many things. You simply didn't think about closing your windows either, when you left." She folded her arms. "And how, may I ask, will we get the car back?" Her voice was oily with sarcasm.

Could this really be happening? All because of the car?

"We'll drive there in the Porsche tomorrow and pick it up." I kept my tone matter-of-fact, trying to calm the waters.

"If they're even open. Tomorrow's Sunday." She turned away. "My own fault, I suppose—I shouldn't have let you persuade me against my better judgment. I only hope major repairs aren't involved."

"Whatever—" I was now so angry that I could hardly speak—"you can deduct it from my wages!"

I hurried upstairs.

Undressing, I saw the beginning of a purple and gold mark on my breast. It no longer hurt, but the memory of the shock and pain were still vivid. Anger at Roy, and now at Paula, too, permeated my entire being.

In bed at last, I reached for a book, thinking I'd calm myself with a quiet read before trying to sleep. The book wasn't there. Strange, I was sure I'd left it here on the night table, with several others. I glanced around. There they were, on the bureau. I must have moved them and forgotten. I got out of bed and found the one I wanted in the tidy pile—then paused, struck by a suspicion. Was it possible—? I went into my living room, where I'd left three days' newspapers on the coffee table. They were gone. I looked in the waste-paper basket, which had been half full. The papers weren't there. The basket had been emptied. A mug and plate that I'd left in the sink had been washed and replaced in the closet.

All thought of sleep vanished. I tore down to the second floor. From outside her room, I could hear the television going. I rapped loudly at the door.

"Come in."

She was sitting propped against the pillows, in darkness except for the light shed by the screen.

"Were you in my rooms?"

"I had to go in to close the windows."

"You moved my things!"

"I tidied up a little, yes. I was quite shocked at the way—"

"This may be your house and I may be your employee, but you have no right to invade my privacy or touch my possessions!"

"It troubles me to see the messy way you—"

"Messy? Two dishes in the sink, a few newspapers—"

"A disordered house means a disordered life! I simply cannot stand—"

"No one's asking you to! I live there, not you! Don't set foot in there again without my permission!"

I went out, slamming the door behind me.

# 7

LEO ARRIVED FOR July Fourth weekend, bringing friends. I'd been apprehensive about the advent of houseguests. Would I be up half the night serving food and drink to the celebrated? Would I be endlessly trundling out to the pool with trays? None of this came to pass, however. Inevitably there were added chores, but the guests were considerate. And I liked the diversion and interest their presence provided. Or perhaps it was just these particular two.

Marcus Cromie wrote books for musicals. Yvonne Lee was a musical comedy singer who had starred in one of Cromie's shows and was soon to tour Europe in *The Merry Widow*. Marcus, Paula told me, had stomach ulcers and needed to eat little but often. Yvonne drank only her own specially bottled water, took a late breakfast, no lunch, and a hearty dinner. Yvonne would only be here for the weekend. Marcus might stay on longer; he was blocked in his work and Leo had suggested that time spent away from the city might prove beneficial.

The morning after they arrived, Marcus came into the kitchen just after seven. He jumped slightly on seeing me. "Oh—er—I wasn't expecting—early riser, aren't you?"

"Yes." I'd begun getting up at six and going for an early dip in the pool before anyone else was around. "Would you like breakfast now?"

"Please. I'd—er—like to take it upstairs. Just coffee. Toast or whatever."

He had salt-and-pepper hair, blunt features, and a smoker's cough. He was wearing now—wore at all times, apparently, for I never saw him in anything else, regardless of time or weather—a grey tweed jacket, from which he didn't bother to brush the ash which fell from his endless cigarettes. He seemed chronically gloomy and fearful; the musicals he wrote must be distinctly downbeat. Yet despite his depressed air and less-than-immaculate grooming, there was something about him . . . a presence, definitely.

He'd been given the daughter's bedroom across the hall from mine because it contained a desk at which he could work. He rarely emerged from this room except to go for solitary walks. When he returned, he immediately went back to work again. From my quarters, I sometimes heard his typewriter going in fits and starts. For a lot of the time, however, there was only silence, punctuated by his cough and by what I thought at first was the sound of him talking to himself, until one night I listened carefully, and realized he was reading aloud passages he was working on.

Yvonne Lee's requirements, too, turned out to be minimal.

"Leave that, I'll do it," she told me, coming in as I made her bed. "I'm sure you've enough to do without extra beds."

Her red hair bounced as she sat down at the dressing table and began to make up. She had a Gibson Girl figure and an effervescent manner; she bubbled all over the place. It could have been too much, but it wasn't. Behind what at first appeared to be froth, I divined a shrewd and sensible person. Towards Paula she was carefully amiable, seeming aware of pitfalls. With Leo and Marcus she was cheerfully noisy and gay, laughing at references only the three of them understood.

Serving dinner the previous evening, I'd heard them discussing some enterprise in which they had all been involved. They'd all been talking at once, interrupting each other, absorbed in what they were saying. Paula sat in silence, watching, head fixed in an attitude of listening, lips curved in a determined smile. Suddenly I'd felt sorry for her. But only for a second. Since that business of the car, we had gone back to Square One with a vengeance. She hadn't deducted the amount of Bloor's bill from my wages, but since then she had spoken to me only to issue some ukase or other. By now, however, this mattered less. Since meeting Graham, my horizons had broadened beyond the house.

Leo came into the kitchen after dinner, while I was cleaning up.

"I thought you might enjoy this." He handed me a book, the autobiography of a famous husband and wife who were actors. "Brand new. I haven't had time to get to it yet. Let me know what you think."

"Have they retired? I haven't heard much about them lately."

"They're working less. Lewis has a heart problem, has to take it easy."

"They were magnificent in *Thunder River*."

"Yes. But *House of Cards* is their own favorite."

"What's this? A powwow?" Yvonne took us in, her eyes lively with curiosity. "I don't mean to interrupt, but I need a lemon."

I gave it to her.

Her glance fell on the book. "I didn't know that was out. I'm dying to read it. Fun to separate fact from fiction!"

"Was Thelma Rund still playing the mother when you saw it, Iris?"

"No. I saw it in Paris." When Oliver had had a show there. Afterwards we had spent a week driving through Brittany. Another lifetime . . .

Paula appeared. "What are you all doing in the kitchen, for goodness' sake? Leo, I wish you'd talk to Marcus, his cigarettes are really getting to be too much . . ."

That night, reading in bed, I looked at the inscription. *For dearest Leo. We embrace you!* The handwriting, like the sentiment, larger than life. Somehow he, too, had picked up that quality. By osmosis, perhaps.

Next morning I went into Yvonne's bathroom to replace the towels. As I came out again, she stopped me. "Tell me, where in the world did Paula find you?"

"Through an employment agency."

"That's not what I mean, as you very well know. Like to hear my theories?" She smiled invitingly.

Who could resist smiling back?

"Number one—" She checked them off on her fingers— "you're hiding out from the FBI. Number two, you're writing an article for a girlie magazine, on the lines of 'What the Housekeeper Saw.' (That's the one Marcus votes for.) Number three—"

Just then, someone rapped at the door.

"Iris, if you can spare a moment, some things require your attention downstairs." Paula's voice was frigid.

"Sorry, Paula, it's my fault, I kept her—"

But Paula had already departed.

In the kitchen she faced me. "You're not paid to stand around talking to my guests!"

It took my breath away. "Your guest initiated the conversation," I said. "And besides—"

"I want the living room done right now. And don't forget to move the sofas and get all the way under this time!" She swept out.

Bitch.

A voice behind me said softly, "Exactly."

God, had I said it aloud?

Marcus went to the sink and took a glass of water. "If I were you, I'd bail out."

• • •

After everyone had finished lunch, I went down to the rocks with a sandwich.

Yvonne, walking the beach in baggy white pants and wide-brimmed straw hat, hailed me. "You look like the Little Mermaid of Copenhagen perched up there."

"Does the Little Mermaid eat tuna fish sandwiches?"

"Pastrami, I'll bet. May I join you?"

"Please."

She climbed up and settled herself. "Just look at that ocean. Too bad it's so blooming cold. I tried it, got as far as my ankles. Now tell me—" She tipped her hat forward to shade her face—"how'd you get trapped by the Wicked Witch of the North?"

I gave her a brief rundown of my checkered career.

She looked meditative. "I've known Leo for years, he handles all my contracts, but I can't say I really know Paula. Is she always like this?"

I struggled to be fair. "Not all the time. Occasionally, she's quite human. Doc Jekyll and Ms. Hyde. Celery?"

She took a stick and munched thoughtfully. "Would you like to get out of here?"

"Out?"

"I mean, quit."

"If I thought I could get something better."

"Of course you can. Why on earth not?"

"I've no degrees, no—ah—significant work history. I can't even type, except with two fingers."

"You could learn to type. Or run a computer. All it takes is practice."

"The thing is, I don't exactly have a good record."

"You mean, you're a felon?"

"It's no joke. I've fallen down on every job I've tried. This was one thing I thought I couldn't mess up. But I'm not terribly sure of that any more, either."

"If this goes wrong, it won't be *your* fault. Why Leo's put up with her all these years is beyond me."

For a while we both stared at the sea in companionable silence.

"Listen, I'm going on tour in September, but meanwhile I'll ask around. You'd be willing to move to New York, wouldn't you, if something offered?"

"Yes. Only—"

"Only what?"

"I wouldn't want to let you down, Yvonne. I warn you, I'm not really a good bet."

For a moment she said nothing. "I don't think you really want another job. You don't want to leave here, do you?"

"Don't want—?"

"Listen to yourself. You undercut yourself at every opportunity."

"That's absurd."

"Is it?" She got to her feet and dusted off her pants. "A word to the wise: if the reason's what I think it is, forget it. He's spoken for."

She clambered down and was gone before I could answer.

I stayed on for a while, watching the waves sigh up the beach with a sibilant hiss. Far out, a lobster boat scooted by, motor coughing.

She was wrong. I wasn't staying because of Leo. Nevertheless, she could easily have been correct. Not once had he been anything but circumspect with me, nor I with him. Still, I'd be lying if I said certain thoughts had never crossed my mind. How could they not, with a man like that? Especially under these circumstances, with an extra fillip added by the *verboten* aspect.

Once, glancing up to find him watching me, I'd jumped.

"Sorry, I didn't mean to startle you. I was just admiring your extreme competence."

"At *this?*" I was putting together Niçoise salad.

"Competence is rare these days, at anything. I admire it wherever I find it."

A good deal more than competent himself, he didn't bother to hide his impatience with ineptitude or mediocrity, meeting it not with cutting remarks but a barely visible shake of the head, taking a mental step away from the miscreant that was almost visible. I'd seen this happen, for example, as Paula's voice ran on . . . Not that he ever rebuked her—publicly, anyway—but it was difficult to miss that mental shrug, that distancing, that almost soundless sigh.

Oh, yes, the implicit flattery of even the smallest compliment from this man might have undone me. Whenever he sought me out to ask the whereabouts of some object, or to discuss some gardening project, he always lingered to talk. Without ever saying so, he made it clear he enjoyed my company. And there were little attentions, various good turns, which he might have done for anyone else in the same situation, I suppose, but which weren't strictly necessary. He had not only installed a good lamp on my desk, but had exchanged my radio for one which got better reception on the public station after we'd talked about a daily news program we both liked. And that book he'd brought me last night had not been a first.

Oh, it was all innocent, yes, but how easily I could have attached significance to these small deeds, could have read meanings into our light exchanges. I was still hurting from Oliver; another man's regard might ease that pain, repair my pride, restore my sexual self-esteem. Especially this man.

Quite often lately, I'd thought of a discussion Joanna and I had once had about men, sex, attraction. Joanna claimed that money was a powerful aphrodisiac. I disagreed. Lots of tycoons were no more exciting than dressmaker dummies, I said. Still, I knew what she meant. It wasn't the money itself, it was the power that money conferred, the deference it brought from others. The thought of someone using that power for *you*, deferring to you in an intimate setting, would have its effect. Even more so when you added brains.

Nevertheless, so far I'd kept my head and, in a manner of speaking, my distance. Even when I'd slightly let down my guard, acted as though we were—almost—flirting acquaintances, there was still nothing to validate what Yvonne had said. Yvonne was wrong.

She was right about something else, however. I ought to have been delighted by her offer. I should have reacted with enthusiasm to the mere idea of a way out of here. Why hadn't I?

On Monday, Leo and Paula had breakfast together, alone. I moved around the table, pouring juice, bringing coffee.

"Leo, I'm going back with you tomorrow for a while. I want to have a talk with Beth, face to face."

He buttered a croissant. "Marcus is staying. Can we leave him?"

"Why not? He's not an infant. In any case, he won't be alone, Iris is here. Anyway, he doesn't need *me*. I don't know that anyone here needs me." Something in her voice.

"Well, fine. I warn you, though, my time's pretty solidly booked."

"That's all right, I have plenty to do. I want to buy some clothes, go to the dentist. I'd like to see that costume show at the Metropolitan. Deedee will go with me, if she's there. If not, I'll go alone. I'm getting used to doing things alone."

He drank some coffee. "What are you planning to say to Beth?"

"That she can't go on like this, throwing her life away. What else can I say?"

"One thing." He pushed back his chair and stood up. "You might tell her to find herself some different friends, or she's going to end up in jail."

"Don't, Leo, you frighten me when—"

There was no one to hear. He had gone.

* * *

He stopped me later as we passed on the stairs. "You'll see the new border gets watered while I'm gone?"

"Yes. Coming along, isn't it?"

"Good to have someone here who has a feeling for these things." From two steps below, he smiled up at me, a smile which seemed to join us in a superior minority. Something in that moment, yes—a certain *frisson*, as they say. "Iris—" He spoke in an undertone—"I know you've a lot to contend with here, but I hope you feel settled. It would mean a great deal to me if—"

"Leo?" The call came shrilly from their bedroom.

She came out on the landing and looked down at us.

For a second, the three of us were utterly still.

"Do you want all the blue shirts, Leo, or—"

"Don't bother, Paula, I'll do my own packing." He went on past me up the stairs.

# 8

SOMEONE TOLD ME once that the man whose real-life experience had inspired *Robinson Crusoe* grew so unused to human contact during his years of involuntary solitude that he was unable to tolerate it. After he came home, he went out to the yard behind his house, dug a hole, and lived in it from thence forward. I kept thinking about that as the date of the playreading approached. Apart from the one evening with Graham, I had had no social activity since leaving Boston. Would I still know how to conduct myself in a group? Or would my social self have withered away for lack of use, past all hope of resuscitation?

I needn't have worried. It seemed I still knew how to behave and converse normally. If anything, I talked too much; I seemed to hear my voice running on. No one seemed to mind, however.

I felt I turned a significant corner that evening. As I took my place in one of the chairs set out for the reading, I felt included as part of that circle. Reborn, as it were, for these people met me not as Harry's former wife, nor Callie's inappropriate mother; not as Oliver's cast-off lover, nor Joanna's weird friend serving a self-imposed sentence of domestic servitude. These people met me as Graham's new friend on whom, by the mere fact of inclusion, he had placed a seal of approval.

The Johnsons, Daphne and Alex, were retired math and

art teachers from Worcester. Alex, professorial, emeritus-looking, beamed a welcome at me. "How nice that Graham discovered you for us." Daphne, white-haired and jolly, had a tendency to salty language. "Shit, Alex, you make it sound as though he found her under a bayberry bush."

Lilly Barzinger, formerly from Jersey, was a laconic string bean of a woman wearing a faded though striking black-and-white print dress of the Thirties and long ropes of glass beads. She gave me a not-unfriendly nod, but hardly spoke. Judgment was being reserved, I felt. Fair enough.

The same went for Jack Fielding, a giant of a man. Hard to tell much about him, disguised as he was by a Smith Brothers beard and metal-rimmed spectacles.

Daphne assigned our roles: Jack was to be Henry Higgins, Lilly was Eliza, Alex doubled as venal Doolittle and sappy Freddy, Daphne was Mrs. and Miss Eynsford-Hill, and Graham was Colonel Pickering.

"Iris, would you please double as Mrs. Higgins and Mrs. Pearce?"

"Mrs. Pearce?"

"The housekeeper."

The reading began and we spoke our lines in those intriguing though sexless roles—Henry with his snobbery and his mother fixation, shameless Doolittle offering his deal, rebellious then tamed-and-trained Eliza. I read my lines as Henry's mother reasonably well, but to the role of Mrs. Pearce, I brought new empathy. Henry, autocrat though he was, would surely be a more congenial employer than Paula Tanner.

Between acts, we broke for wine and cheese and conversation. At the end of the evening, Lilly asked for my phone number. "I'll call you." Off-handed. I knew about that kind of invitation.

The Johnsons, however, fixed an actual date. "Saturday? Sunday, then. Good. Bring your swimsuit, we're on a pond."

Jack bade me a polite good-night, donned a Greek 'fisherman's cap, and pedalled away on his bicycle.

At Graham's invitation, I stayed on for a final glass of wine after the others had left. Together we restored the shop to order, taking out chairs, wiping up crumbs, washing glasses.

"You were a hit, Iris, everyone took to you. I knew they would."

He sounded like Henry with Eliza.

"Look at the time, where *is* that boy? I specifically asked him not to be late. We have to get up early to do inventory tomorrow."

Not eager to encounter that boy, I took my leave. As I drove home, I reviewed the evening. More than one person in this group resembled Eliza; except possibly for Graham, each seemed to have gone through, or still be going through, some kind of metamorphosis. Daphne and Alex were now weaver and nature photographer respectively. Jack, an organic chemist with a Ph.D., was now a metalsmith. Lilly Barzinger had been a public health nurse and now ran an antiques business, Lilly's Treasures. Nor was it only a matter of career change; all these people, like me, came not only from other places but a different way of living. Unlike them, however, I'd gone down in the world—from wife, mother, and varsity scarlet letter to paid domestic. *Quo vadis, Iris?*

Three days later, Jack Fielding called and invited me out for a bicycle ride.

"I thought we'd head for Grey's Point, about eight miles from here. There's a café nearby where we can get something to eat."

I said there was one problem: no bicycle.

He could borrow a bicycle from one of his housemates, he said. "How's ten o'clock? That way we have a chance of beating the weather." It had rained almost every afternoon lately.

"I'm sorry, I can't get away before one."

"Okay. We'll keep our fingers crossed."

From first moment to last, the excursion was a disaster. It began to rain the minute we passed the point of no return, and didn't let up for the rest of the day. I hadn't ridden a bicycle for years, and when I had to keep stopping to take a breather, Jack grew impatient. "If you'll just bend forward a little more—"

"My back's sore, so's my seat. Every muscle in my legs aches. What's more, that truck soaked me with spray!"

When we finally reached Grey's Point, everything was shrouded in mist. Visions of hot chocolate danced in my head. "Where did you say that place was? The café?"

The café turned out to be closed.

By the time we got back to Jack's house, I never wanted to see a bicycle again. "Where do you want this infernal machine?"

"Leave it there, I'll take care of it. Come in for a drink. I'll start a fire, get you warm and dry. You look like a drowned rabbit." He sounded amused.

That did it. "I feel like one, too! Not my idea of fun!" I flared. "Thanks, anyway, about the drink." Soaked to the skin, sore of leg, back, and crotch, I limped to the car and drove away. So much for that beautiful friendship.

A week after Paula and Leo had left for New York, I drove Marcus to the airport. Now that his work was completed, he was eager to get back to the city. He kept fidgeting as we drove, worrying that he would miss his flight, though we'd left in plenty of time. "I don't like this fog," he muttered.

"Don't worry, it'll all be gone in half an hour."

I'd enjoyed his being at the house. He had stayed at work most of the time, but when he emerged, he seemed to want company. He'd joined me several times in my early morning dips. Once we took a long walk around the headland near Wixsey Light. Yesterday afternoon, after he'd finally finished, he'd suggested we go out to celebrate. "Would you—er—like to try that fish place near the wharf?"

Off we'd gone to dinner, then to see *Carousel* at the Music Box.

"You seem sad," he said, as I drove us home.

I was. *Carousel* had released a flood of memory. *If I loved you, Time and again I would try to say, All I'd want you to know* . . . But it wasn't Oliver I'd been thinking about. It was Callie, who'd played Julie in a high school production. Sitting beside Marcus in the darkened theatre, I'd closed my eyes, hearing the slight break in Callie's youthful treble, seeing Callie in the calico dress, a black velvet ribbon tying back her hair. Harry and I had thought her wonderful. Harry had taken numerous photographs during the performance. Backstage afterwards, Callie had been in seventh heaven, excited as I'd never seen her by the praise and applause. That night, while Callie went on to a cast party, Harry and I, united for once in our roles as proud parents, went home and made love.

All at once, I'd found myself grieving, longing, not for Harry but for what we had all three been on that long-ago evening, a family joined in rare harmony.

"It reminded me of my daughter, when she was younger."

We began to talk, cautiously exchanging some personal history. It was then I learned that Marcus had been married and divorced four times.

"That's it. Four times and out. I've had my quota." He sounded relieved. He now lived part of the time in a residential hotel in Manhattan, and the rest visiting friends.

On our way to the airport, he made me an extraordinary offer.

"Time to talk business, Iris. You can't go on much longer with this—er—ridiculous charade."

"Charade? It's called earning a living, Marcus."

He snorted.

All right for him, with his multi-marriages and royalties and trouble-free residence in a good hotel.

"Not much in the way of jobs around here, I'd say. You'll need to go to—er—Boston or New York or wherever to look. While you look, you'll need money."

"Money?"

"I'll stake you."

"Stake—?"

"Must you keep echoing every word I say?"

"Marcus, are you offering me *money?*"

"A cushion, while you—er—look around."

"That's very generous, Marcus, but I couldn't possibly—"

"Why not? You need it, I have it. Here's where to reach me when you're ready."

He took out a card and tucked it in my pocket.

"Marcus, you're very kind, but I can't accept—"

"Don't be silly. What's money for? Only, don't delay. Go soon."

Something in the way he said it.

"Why? Is there a special reason?"

"Time's a-wasting, that's all. Ah, here we are. Good. Don't bother—er—to park, just let me off."

He leaned over and gave me an avuncular kiss, then departed.

I watched him walk away, bag in one hand, briefcase bulky with manuscript in the other. I felt touched by his offer. I'd miss our conversations, and the sound of his typewriter tapping far into the night. I'd miss the sight of that grey-clad figure wreathed in cigarette smoke, resembling some ancient deity rising through clouds. Just for a moment I wondered what his wives had been like.

It felt as though I were on vacation, staying as a guest in this luxurious hotel, living free in return for providing my own services. Mornings, as a sop to Cerberus, I made a desultory pass at the chores. At noon, I downed tools and spent the rest of the time as I chose, taking off wherever and whenever the spirit moved.

I spent time with Daphne and Alex in their house on Willett Pond. The house was crammed to bursting with evidence of their pursuits. Not hobbies, these. Daphne's work was shown in galleries and sold in craft shops. Alex's photographs appeared in shows and magazines. Boxes of prints and negatives, paper and chemicals, paper cutters, framing supplies, were everywhere; the darkroom was in the cellar. Daphne's studio upstairs contained her loom; deep shelves along the wall held the fruit of her labors—wallhangings and fabrics and items made from those fabrics. Just now she and Alex were assembling work for a joint show.

As we tramped around the pond, and swam, and later ate a picnic meal on the patio Alex had built, I found myself watching these two, and listening. Clearly they were pleased with each other, each the other's best friend and booster. It could have been smug, faintly irritating, but it wasn't. It was possible, then, to reach this stage of life in tandem and in good repair, emotionally as well as physically?

I turned out to be wrong about Lilly. She called not long after the playreading and asked me over.

Lilly's Treasures was located in a barn-like structure. The treasures consisted of furniture, bric-a-brac, picaresque clothing, and junk jewelry. Every item seemed worn, decrepit, or in disrepair, if not actually moldy. Dust hung like a scrim in the shadowy recesses, which were wanly illuminated by a few naked bulbs hanging from the rafters. Everything was stored in great higgledy-piggledy piles, ceiling-high in some places. I asked Lilly why she didn't arrange it in some kind of order, make it more accessible. She gave me a pitying look for my ignorance. "When people have to dig for it, they feel they'll stumble on bargains." There *were* bargains, if you were prepared to put in time searching, had the strength to extricate whatever you wanted, and were willing to invest further hours repairing and refinishing.

Her house, like its owner, was tall and narrow. The interior, too, was rather like Lilly, with her brave ropes of beads—unusual, a little shabby, but with pizzazz. No rugs? No matter. Each floor was painted a different primary color. The threadbare curtains had clearly once been the finest lace. The doorknobs tended to come off in your hand, but *such* doorknobs—of cut glass, embossed brass, painted porcelain. The intricate carving on the heavy stairpost was a marvel.

Lilly was proficient in ways which evoked my deepest admiration. On my first visit I'd arrived to find her perched at the top of a thirty-foot ladder, doing something to one of the eaves of the house. A squirrel had been chewing up there; she was fixing screening over the spot to deter further damage. "Almost through," she called. Minutes later, she scampered down with the confidence of a trapeze artist. She herself had built the low stone wall that surrounded her property. Her latest project was automotive maintenance; she was currently learning how to pull a transmission.

She said very little about her personal life on that first visit. No husband or lover was mentioned or in evidence. Did she live alone? Was she single, divorced, widowed? She didn't say. Only quite a long time afterwards did she mention that she was going away for a few days, taking the ferry to Nova Scotia. To do what? "To see Victor." "Who's Victor?" "My husband." "Lilly, you're married?" She nodded. "But then—" "Oh, Lord, we don't live together. I couldn't stand it. We visit back and forth, though."

In her kitchen I noticed a brochure taped to the refrigerator, listing adult education courses at the community college in the next town. It turned out Lilly taught a furniture refinishing course there one night a week.

"Anything there interest you?"

I studied it. The art of bonsai. Easy Esperanto. Baking with verve. Tai Chi. Here was something: Computer Scan. *For*

*those who are new to computers or who have limited experience.*
That would be feet-on-the-ground, wouldn't it? Eight weeks,
seventy-five dollars. Tuesday nights at seven. Term started
September eighth. Why not?

"Good, that's my night too," Lilly said. "We can ride
together. You come right past here on the way."

At intervals Paula telephoned. Was the house all right?
(No, someone stole it while I was out at the store.) Was
there any mail? (Two bills and a coupon special for seniors.)
Important messages? (Annabelle's had the yarn she needed.)
Nothing else? (Was she expecting word from the Queen of
Ruritania?)

Over the phone she seemed to unbend somewhat. They
had had dinner with Marcus, who reported I'd taken excellent
care of him. "I must say, Iris, you seem to have made an
impression." New York was unbelievably hot, but she was
going to stay on for a while longer, until Leo could come
back—she couldn't abandon him while he was working so
hard.

# 9

WITH PAULA'S ABSENCE EXTENDED, I decided to repay some
of the hospitality I'd been enjoying.

For a start, I invited Graham to dinner, hoping he wouldn't
assume that Roy was included. Fortunately he made no such
assumption. He said Roy had plans for the evening and
needed the car, so he would drop Graham off and collect
him later.

Roy let Graham off at the appointed time and drove away
at once, to my great relief. I showed Graham around the
house, then we went to the beach to watch the sunset.
Afterwards, while the trees turned to black cutouts against
the dusk, we had dinner on the deck, by candlelight.

Soon after ten, there was the sound of a car pulling up.
The doorbell sounded. "That'll be Roy." Graham followed
as I went to the door.

"Howdy." Roy gave me his smile.

Flanking him, like bookends or bodyguards, were two men
who stared at me silently.

"Why—hello, Pete, Giorgio." Graham seemed less than
delighted to see them.

The one in black leather pants and vest nodded back. He
looked albino, with those bleached eyes, white hair and skin.
The one in satin jeans and leopardskin tank top ignored him.

"Man!" Roy walked past us, followed by the others. "Some
joint!" Uninvited, they took themselves on a tour.

"Just a minute—" I hurried after them, uncomfortably aware that I was officially in charge. If anything happened to this house or anything in it, I'd be held responsible. But they touched nothing, only wandered from room to room, looking.

"Crikey!" Roy had caught sight of the piano. He went over and played a chord. "How about I come by and use this when I'm writing?"

"Roy, we have to be going," Graham said.

"What's the rush?" He sat down and ran a scale. "Good news, Baxie—I'm starting at Showplace Fridays and Saturdays."

Graham's face lit up. "That's wonderful, Roy! Isn't it wonderful, Iris?"

Roy launched into a song, while Black Leather stretched out full length on the sofa and Satin Jeans patrolled the edges of the room.

Don't worry. They're probably outstanding citizens, kind to children and dogs. But if something happens—? Nothing will happen. Stop fussing.

*Gonna take to the road,* Roy sang. *You come along, too . . . I'll show you a real good time . . . At the end of the road . . .*

Black Leather lay motionless, arms dangling. Had he died? Satin Jeans was crouching on the hearth, inspecting the great glass bowl filled with pebbles.

*Skip the highways, find the byways . . . Make our getaway the better way . . .*

Suddenly, over the music came a sound that froze my blood: the doorbell.

I stood transfixed. Surely she'd have called to have me pick her up? Or had she deliberately planned this, dropping in without notice?

Again the doorbell.

Graham turned. "Isn't that—"

I nodded, unable to utter, and went to the door.

"You certainly took your time!" She stepped in and put down her suitcase.

Paula's voice—but not Paula. It was the photo in Paula's den come to life. The drifting daughter.

*Ain't no lies told . . . at the end of the road . . . Ain't no fool's gold . . . at the end of the road . . .*

"What's that?"

In that small pouty face surrounded by bushy hair, those tilted eyes were arresting.

"A friend of mine is just—"

But she had already gone past me and into the living room. Roy, still singing, was oblivious. So was Black Leather. Satin Jeans gave her a cursory glance and lost interest.

Now Graham saw her. He glanced from her to me and back to her again. She ignored us, her attention on Roy.

After what seemed an eternity, the song ended.

"Roy—" Graham moved forward and spoke urgently. "We have to be going!"

At last Roy turned and saw her. "Hey, there!" He smoothed his curls and gave her his smile. "Who're you?"

"I might ask you the same." She studied him coolly. Above her white jeans, the pink shirt knotted at her midriff revealed a triangle of golden flesh.

"Name's Roy." He closed the piano lid, carefully. "Lead guitar, from Serpent."

"Serpent?"

"My band." He went and stood in front of her, feet astride, thumbs in his pockets. "Drop by Showplace some time. I'll be doing songs from my album."

"Roy!" Graham's face had reddened with distress. "We simply must—"

"Okay, Baxie, keep your shirt on." He looked at Beth. "See you around."

He left, trailed by Graham and cohorts. I felt weak with relief as the door closed after them.

"Well! You've been having quite a party!"

"Not exactly. My friend Graham came over. Roy came to pick him up, that's all."

"Who were the others?"

"Friends of Roy's, I suppose. No one I know."

She let it drop. "I guess I'll go up and get settled."

She took her suitcase and went upstairs. I went out to the deck to clear the dishes.

Almost immediately, she was down again. "Someone's been sleeping in my bed!"

"Your—?" Then I realized. "A friend of your parents was using that room. I haven't tidied up in there since he left."

"Oh?" She gave me a slow, knowing smile. "Don't worry about it, I'll sleep in my mother's room. I like the big bed anyway." She followed me to the kitchen. "Anything to eat?"

"Eggs, cheese, cold chicken. Help yourself."

She took food from the refrigerator while I loaded the dishwasher. "Any more tomatoes?"

"Down the bottom." Dare I ask how long she intended to stay? "Your mother won't be back for—"

"I know. I spoke to her yesterday. I'm just going to hang out for a while."

While I washed the pots, emptied the trash, and wiped off the counter, she sat and ate. Finally she put down her fork and leaned back, yawning. "That hit the spot. Time for beddy-byes, I'm pooped." She walked out, leaving her dishes on the table.

I suppose it was unreasonable to resent her presence; this was her parents' house, after all, not mine. But my ire grew over the next few days as I picked up her dishes, collected sandals, bandanas, and tape player from the deck, towels strewn by the pool, drinking glasses from everywhere. The first morning, I'd gone reluctantly into her room—Paula's room—from which she had finally emerged at noon. For a second I'd stood still, appalled; how could she so quickly have managed to transform this stark preserve into such a scene of disarray? I was no doubt obliged to make the bed and do the bathroom, but must I also pick up the undies flung hither and yon, the magazines and other items scattered everywhere? Reluctantly, I'd begun to do so when her voice sounded sharply behind me. "What are you doing in here?"

"I came to make the bed and—"

"Stay out. I don't want you touching my things."

"Fine with me!"

I walked out, cheeks burning.

She usually stayed up half the night watching television, and slept till at least noon or one o'clock the following day. Even after she got out of bed, she spent most of her time horizontal, lying on the deck or by the pool or prone on the sofa. Often a sweetish smell hovered in the air around her; her speech was alternately slow, then fast and excitable, words tumbling over each other, interspersed with pointless laughter. The cause was obvious, but she was not my responsibility, thank goodness.

Yet as time passed, I found I didn't mind her that much after all. If she had been *my* daughter, her sloth, apathy, and drugs would have driven me to fury. Since she wasn't, and since she didn't impose herself or make special demands, her easygoing ways and lack of self-discipline didn't particularly bother me. I found them preferable to her mother's obsessiveness.

In fact, after the first few days, she came to seem like company, though we didn't exchange much in the way of conversation. I was curious about her—Paula's daughter. Knowing more about the daughter might tell me more about the mother.

Something else further prompted my curiosity: inevitably, I kept comparing her with Callie.

One thing I'd decided the night she arrived: her presence wasn't going to deter me from any plans of my own. While she lay around semi-comatose from drugs, or just generally out of it, I went about my own business, wherever, whenever. I went into town. I saw my friends. I went with Lilly and her helper, Skoota, a snaggle-toothed fellow with a pickup truck, on buying trips to house sales. I went to dinner at the Johnsons and met some friends of theirs, Sue and Frank Wenzel, a young, athletic-looking couple, physicians who had moved here from Connecticut to practice family medicine. I went with Graham one night to a Souza concert in Tiscat. My ticket, I gathered, had been intended for Roy, who turned out to be otherwise engaged.

On her fifth day, Beth came in from the deck in her bikini, flopped down in a chair at the kitchen table, and yawned hugely. "What a drag this place is. Nothing to do. How do you stand it?"

"Care to polish a floor? Wash a few windows? Do a little laundry?"

She gave me a look.

"If you find it so dull, why did you come?" I asked.

"I needed a place to crash, that's why." She chewed on a hangnail. "I had to give up my apartment. My landlord had his eye on my lily-white bod, but I wouldn't come across so he made up some story."

Could a tenant be evicted for drug use? If so, surely half the city's population would be camped on the sidewalk. "How much longer will you be here?"

"What's it to you?"

"I'm doing the food shopping today. If you're staying—"

"I don't know. A week, maybe two." She twined a finger in her curly hair. "Think I'll take a ride, look up some people."

"I'll need the wagon for shopping."

"Okay. I'll take the Porsche."

"Have you the key?"

"No. Don't you?"

"No."

"Come on!"

"For me, the Porsche is off limits. I just work here, re-member?"

She suddenly smiled, with a hint of mischief. "Guess we're second-class citizens, you and me. We'll have to ride together, that's all."

She went upstairs and came back wearing jeans and a red silk T-shirt which I recognized as her mother's. A silver bangle, also her mother's, encircled her wrist.

We went out to the car. "Do you want to drive?" I asked, and instantly regretted the offer.

She shrugged. "I don't care. You can."

While I drove, she turned on the radio, loud.

"Would you mind turning that down a little, please?"

With a gesture of impatience, she turned it down and stared out the window, humming to the music.

In profile, her sullen expression was softened, she looked younger, less knowing. There was something appealing about her, despite everything. A pity she seemed so shiftless. As a parent, I could feel some sympathy with the Tanners. Harry and I had been fortunate in this respect, anyway.

"What was the name of that guy?" she asked.

"Who?"

"The one playing the piano the other night."

"Oh." I slowed at a stop light. "Roy."

"Roy what?"

"I don't know."

Perhaps he didn't even have a second name. Perhaps he was one of that breed—martyrs, magicians, or rock stars—for whom a single name suffices.

"Is he a friend of yours?"

"No indeed. Of Graham's." The light changed and I pulled away.

"Ever hear him play guitar?"

"Yes."

"Any good?"

"To my surprise, yes."

"Why surprise?" she wanted to know.

A valid question. Could I say, Because of what he is and the way he lives. Because he's a parasite, leeching off Graham, using Graham until the next free ride comes along.

"You're right," I said. "Talent hasn't much to do with character. Where do you want me to drop you off?"

"Uh-uh, I'll drop *you*. I'm keeping the car."

She let me off at the market. We arranged that she'd pick me up at four at a nearby café called Juke's. If I got through early or if she were delayed, I could sit there and have a cup of coffee while I waited. I'd leave the groceries at the market; we'd collect them when she arrived.

At four-forty I was still waiting at Juke's. Not that I minded. It was pleasant sitting at an outdoor table, sipping espresso, watching people go by. Idly I leafed through a *Times* that someone had left on the low brick wall surrounding the patio. I turned another page and a name jumped out at me.

In shock, I read the story, stared at the picture that went with it. A conventionally pretty face, with conventional name to match. Susan. A stockbroker. Daughter of, grand-daughter of, previous marriage ended in divorce. Why did they never print the groom's picture, only the vital statistics? A painter, most recent show was, son of, grandson of the late. I felt as though I'd been punched hard in the solar plexus.

"Iris!"

I looked up. There she stood, laughing, saying something.

". . . espresso? I'll have one, too. Sorry I'm late." She giggled. "I met some people . . ."

For the life of me, I couldn't make out what she was saying. Some kind of sound barrier seemed to garble the words. A strange pain had begun in my chest—a dull ache, like a headache that had slipped. The beginning of a heart

attack? Consumption? Something that would mercifully carry
me off?

"What's the matter? Got the blues?" She tipped her head
to one side, watching. "Want something to chase those blues
away?" One eyelid closed, meaningly.

Thanks, you choose your drug, I'll choose mine. Say, a
stiff double Scotch. "Beth—I'd like to go home." Amazing,
how lips, tongue, larynx all seemed to work. "I'm . . .
expecting a call."

"Okay." She drank the last mouthful and gave me a witless,
dazzling smile. "All done."

"I'm driving," she announced.

I was in no mood to argue. I leaned my head back and
closed my eyes as we sped erratically along.

All this time, I finally acknowledged, I must have been
nursing a secret fantasy: Oliver would have a change of heart,
fly up here and carry me off. *Oh, young Lochinvar is come
out of the West, Through all the wide Border his steed was the
best* . . . Who was this Susan, with her Dow Jones averages,
her over-the-counter offerings, her traded commodities? Could
a stockbroker and a painter find happiness together? A nasty
little voice deep inside me whispered, You bet.

"Okay, end of the line, everyone out!" Beth announced.

Getting out, I saw that she had run the front wheel over
the new border, crushing the ageratum and dusty miller.

The telephone was ringing as we walked in. Beth picked
it up. "Hello?" Like a kitten's purr. "Oh." Her voice changed.
"We were in town, doing the marketing. What? I don't know.
Ask Dad, why don't you, he's the resident expert." She gave
a loud, exaggerated sigh. "Yes, I know. You've told me. I
don't *care* what he thinks." Her voice grew shrill. "You can
tell him from me he's in no position to preach!" She slammed
down the receiver. "Some joke, lecturing *me*, while she—"

Again the telephone rang.

"If that's her, I've gone out!" She rushed from the room.

"Iris? Put Beth on the line, please." Paula sounded agitated.

"She's gone out."

"Oh? When will she be back?"

"She didn't say."

"Tell her to call me when she comes back, please. Is everything all right there?"

What did that mean? "Yes. Fine."

"By the way, if you run short of household money, there's some extra cash in the drawer in my night table. Iris—" She paused. "Keep an eye on everything. Will you?"

I knew what she meant. But I was no babysitter and Beth was no baby. Anyway, it was the kind of favor you'd ask of a friend or a long-time employee with whom you were on personal terms, not something she could expect of the kind of servant she'd insisted I be. Ask me no favors, Mrs. Tanner.

After we'd hung up, I went straight upstairs and poured myself a full tumbler of Scotch. Followed by another. And another. That should do it.

Then I undressed and got into bed. Come to think of it, we hadn't picked up the groceries. As I lay there, I heard the telephone begin to ring. Let the telephone ring, let the groceries rot, let Oliver go for broke with his broker.

*Ladybird, ladybird, fly away home, your maid is crocked, your daughter is stoned.*

I pulled the sheet over my face and passed blessedly into unconsciousness.

# 10

SOMEONE RAPPED AT THE DOOR. "Iris?" The voice seemed
to come from far in the distance. "Iris? Are you awake?"

With effort, I unglued my eyelids. Slowly the ceiling tilted,
then righted itself.

Beth's face swam towards me. Her voice, close now, said
*"Finally."*

I pulled myself to a sitting position. "Just because I sleep
in a little—"

"I'll say. It's three o'clock. P.M. Are you okay?"

I started to nod, then reconsidered as a hammer struck
inside my temple.

She sat down on the bed. "I'm going for a swim—a real
one, in the ocean. Want to come?"

Ugh.

"Come on. It'll do you good, wake you up."

It would at that. Perhaps I should. *Gonna wash that man
right outa my hair.* Not so simple, alas. Still, it would certainly
rouse me out of this stupor.

With infinite care I slowly moved my feet to the floor,
then sat still, waiting for everything to settle down.

"I need coffee first."

"I've made some." Did I hear that right? "Come on down
when you're ready."

• • •

She seemed in exceptionally good spirits, unaided by chemistry, so far as I could tell. Or did she just seem that way in contrast to my own state?

When we got to the beach, she started running and hit the surf so fast I couldn't have caught up with her even if I'd tried. I wasn't about to. Going slowly, I managed to get in as far as my knees, then halted, all my system shocked with cold. How could she stand it? I stood watching her, shading my eyes with my hand. Already she was quite a long way out, moving along in a stylish crawl.

Now she turned and headed back. "Chicken!" Her voice came faintly across the water.

Inch by inch, I ventured forward. I'd never make it this way. *Now.* Holding my breath, I plunged, and seconds later was moving through the water till we were level with each other. Now we trod water, both of us laughing, as though we'd accomplished something clever. She wore no cap; her rambunctious hair, flattened by the water, clung sleekly.

I suddenly thought of Callie at Wellfleet, four years old, hair floating on the water as she lay back, propped on her hands, at the water's edge. "Watch! I'm thwimming!" she would shriek in delight.

How easy it had been to please Callie in those days, to make her happy. How simple everything had been back then. Nowadays nothing was simple, everything was incredibly complicated. Callie, I'm sorry, for whatever I did to hurt you. God knows I never meant to.

The least I could do for Callie now was not drag her down with my problems, my sorrows. Joanna was right: I'd been a dead weight on Callie. It was time to change. This very evening, I'd write Callie a cheerful letter for once, mentioning no problems, asking no favors. I'd even enclose a modest check towards what I owed her. Lately I'd sent out a number of such checks, albeit minuscule, to various people from whom I'd borrowed. I'd show her I was managing, was learning at last to take care of myself. It was true, wasn't

it? Here I was, staying afloat, despite everything, even that
news in yesterday's paper—alive and, if not exactly kicking,
surviving.

Surviving! A tiny flame of self-approval all at once sparked
into being. A current of energy surged through me. I swum
a vigorous survivor's swim around Beth, feeling new strength
as I stroked along, arms and legs propelling me cleanly
through the water. Afloat!

"I'm going in," Beth called.

"Me too."

Together we swam back to shore and toweled off. Beth's
hair stood out in an aureole. Her face glowed from the water.
"Feels good, doesn't it?"

"Yes." I was shivering but tingling. I felt different, as
though I'd shed an old skin. I felt cleansed, purged, as though
I'd come through some kind of test. I was managing, wasn't
I? I'd held on here through some difficult times, and I'd
made some friends, and I was slowly whittling down the
National Debt. As for the latest news that *The Times* considered fit to print, that too I could cope with. In time.

Experimentally, I spoke his name to myself.

*Oliver.*

It hurt—but here I stood nevertheless, breathing, inhaling
the tang of the sea, feeling the cool air on my skin, the gritty
beach beneath my feet. I stared down. Each grain was the
result of processes going back to the beginning of earth itself.
Try to see it in that context, the larger picture, till the pain
grows small, tiny, infinitesimal, less significant than any of
these.

It was tranquil, out on the deck. We had put on sweat
shirts and pants, and I was enjoying the feeling of being
cosy and dry after our swim. The air was perfectly still, as
it always was just before dusk. The light was strangely
beautiful as day barely began to merge into evening. In this
light Beth's sloe eyes were velvety black in that golden face.

Her legs were crossed; one foot swung back and forth, back and forth, sandal dangling.

"Ever go on a ferris wheel, Iris?"

"Uh-uh. I don't like heights."

"It's thrilling. I haven't been on one for years. My father used to take me. He liked it too. We'd hang on to each other and yell like crazy as we reached the top. Anyway—"

"Anyway, what?"

"Oh, I was just thinking. My life feels like that sometimes. Some days I'm right at the top, I can look down and see the whole world spread out. Other times, boy, I'm down deep. You know?"

"Oh, yes. I seem to be stuck in the middle lately."

She wrinkled her nose. "Dull."

"A big improvement on stuck at the bottom, let me tell you."

"Iris, what's your daughter like?" Her face grew serious with interest, as though she really did want to know.

How to describe Callie?

"Smart. Pretty. On her way up. She's a lawyer."

"Is she older than me?"

"A few years younger."

"Are you and she pretty close?"

I hesitated. "We were. Then we weren't. I think—"

The sound of the telephone cut me off. I picked up. "Hello?"

"Irene? Lemme speak to Beth."

Wrong number? Get lost? She's gone to China? "For you, Beth." Did she hear the distress in my voice?

"Hi, there . . ." Her lips curved in a smile. "Call you right back," she said softly, hung up, and went indoors.

I sat there wondering, worrying, as darkness came on. Through the darkness I could hear the gulls' shrill clamor. I could hear the distant thunder of the sea as it launched itself against the rocks.

Beth returned and flicked on the light. "I'm going out soon.

I'll need the car." She didn't say where she was going and I didn't ask. No need. "If you have to go out, I'll drop you off, but you'll have to get your own way home."

I should say something, try to dissuade her. But what?

"I feel like a drink. Some wine." She went away, came back bringing a bottle and glasses. "Dear old Dad's finest!" Laughing, she flashed the label.

I was aghast. "Beth, that's a very—"

"You only live once, as the actress said to the bishop." She filled a glass, held it out.

"No, thanks."

"You're my guest. I'm inviting you!"

"I don't want any, Beth. Thank you."

She shrugged. "Suit yourself." She sipped, then sighed with contentment. "Can I ask you something personal, Iris?"

"Ask away."

"How did you happen to end up here? I mean—"

"I know what you mean." I delivered the cautionary tale in a few bald sentences: I left my husband for someone else, who then changed his mind. Leaving me high and dry, sans him, sans money. So here I am.

It sounded more like soap opera each time I told it. On the other hand, what about *Anna Karenina*? Things would have turned out differently for Anna today, no doubt. For one thing, she'd probably have won joint custody of her child. For another, she'd probably still be happy with Vronsky, or without him, while busily pursuing her career as a civil engineer or social worker. The one thing I couldn't see her doing was working as someone's maid. Therein lay the difference, I suppose, between Tolstoy and soap opera. How typical of me to get stuck with the lead in *A Brighter Tomorrow*.

"But why here?" Beth persisted. "Anyone who works for my mother has to be crazy."

"Or desperate. We aren't all fortunate enough to live on parental bounty," I said, tartly.

Her face changed. "Who are you to lecture me?"

"Who are you to decide I'm crazy?"

For a second we stared at each other like cats engaged in a hissing match.

"Okay, I get your message. Anyway, I didn't mean it like that. I just meant, she's so awful, how can—"

"Don't do that!"

"Do what?"

"Run her down. To me."

"Since when are you such a fan?"

"I'm not, but she's my employer. It puts me in a difficult position. Like that." I pointed to the wine.

"That's my father's wine, isn't it? Can't I drink his wine?"

"*You* can, maybe. Not me. Not that wine, anyway."

She seemed to consider, then shrugged.

"She's such a patsy, that's all. Telling me how to live my life while she behaves like a total wimp."

A wimp? *Paula*? Caligula's sister, Attila's mother, was more like it.

"All that crap about how happy she is, what a perfect marriage she has. He screws every young actress around! The latest one is twenty-three!"

As soon as she said it, I knew I had known. The gist, anyway. "Perhaps she doesn't know," I offered cautiously.

"She knows, all right! Everyone knows. She'd have to be deaf, dumb, and blind."

Or putting a blind eye to the telescope. You pays your money and takes your choice: how much pain is it worth to preserve the status quo by pretending not to see? To Paula, it was worth a lot, apparently.

"Hypocrites, both of them."

Like Callie, she saw it in such simple terms, so clear-cut black-and-white. Still, the pain produced was just as real. Tears stood in her eyes. "Looks at me as though I'm dirt. He says I disgust him." All at once she was weeping.

I put an arm around her. "Callie, your father didn't mean—" On the other hand, perhaps he did. God only knew under what circumstances he'd used those words. "It's frustration, that's all, because you and he can't—"

She pulled violently away, brushed at her eyes, jumped to her feet. "Seven-thirty!" She hurried indoors.

When she came back, she had changed to white jeans and Paula's mauve silk shirt. Paula's heavy choker of beaten gold was around her throat. Her bruised-looking mouth was a glossy crimson, her eyes gleamed through sooty shadow. "Ta-ra-rah! How do I look?" She struck a pose, hand on her hip.

"Delicious." A tasty morsel, he'll chew you up, spit you out. "Beth. Pass this one up. He's bad news."

She opened her eyes very wide, an innocent. "Who?"

"You know very well."

"Hey, listen, you're not exactly my guar-dee-yan, you know. Anyway—" She smiled. "I don't find him bad news at all. If you get my drift."

I gave up. "Do you have a key?"

"Yes, Mama!" She laughed jeeringly. "I think you're mixing me up with your daughter."

"Pardon *me*," I said coldly.

"Forget it." She started to leave. At the last second, she looked back. "Basically, life is just a bowl of crud, n'est ce pas?"

*Dear Brenda, Here's a tiny installment towards what I owe. I'm grateful for your patience . . .*

*Dear Ruth and Carl, The enclosed comes with my deepest thanks . . .*

*Dear Linda, Herewith a small payment . . .*

As I wrote, faint strains of Forties dance music drifted in through my window—Artie Shaw, Harry James, Benny Goodman. Someone was having an outdoor party, with a band. I could hear not only the music but the sound of voices scrambled by distance into a low hubbub, punctuated at times by a shriek of laughter or a cry of greeting. I could picture the scene down to the last detail. All the women would be good-looking, or would seem so, golden in their airy summer dresses; all the men would sound hearty, infused with well-being from their days devoted to tennis, sailing, and golf and an appetite stimulated by sea air and a slight edge of boredom.

I'd attended similar parties myself, in my former life. If I wanted to crash this party, I knew exactly how I'd do it. First, I'd dress appropriately—in my blue Marimekko, say, with white coin dots. Then I'd make my appearance and advance with confidence, *toujours* confidence, the key to success, smiling easily as I mingled. If anyone asked me who I was, I'd sing my name out blithely. Confidence was the entire secret, in all things—walk the tightrope, don't look down, you'll make it.

I thought of my friend Natasha, an excellent tennis player, who almost always lost, however, because nerves overcame her ability to concentrate. One day Natasha's life changed: her son fell ill, at fifteen. Natasha stopped playing for the year of his illness, started again after his death. She won nearly all the time now. Someone asked her why. "Tennis became unimportant," she said. "I stopped worrying about what happened on the court." After what had happened off the court.

Once more the telephone. Paula checking up?

I was wrong. It was Leo.

"Iris, this is a quick call, I'm in kind of a hurry. Is Beth there?"

"She's gone out."

"You gave her the message to call home, I take it?"

"Of course."

"Has she by any chance asked you for money?"

"Asked *me*? No."

"If she does, I'd be obliged if you wouldn't give it to her."

"That's easy. I'm hardly in a position—"

"But Paula says she left cash there, for expenses. Three hundred dollars."

Right. I'd forgotten. "I haven't needed it so far. It must still be in the bedroom."

"Get it, will you please? And put it somewhere safe until you need it. I'm sorry to bother you with this family imbroglio. Thanks for holding the fort."

He hung up just as the band swung into *Moonlight in Vermont.*

I switched on the lamp in Paula's room.

The bed was unmade. Garments were everywhere. Paula's yellow kimono patterned with butterflies lay on the floor. A sandal stood on the dressing table, along with a glass containing ancient-looking dregs. A bureau drawer stood wide, lingerie spilling out. Minimal panties hung over a lamp, a halter top dangled from a doorknob. Magazines lay everywhere.

I picked my way through the detritus to the bedside table. In the drawer were a nail file and something flat wrapped in tissue paper. No money. Had it somehow got pushed to the back? I checked. Not there. The flat object in tissue didn't feel like money but—I unwrapped it. *Alice in Wonderland.* I shook out the pages, which were brittle with age. Out fell a photograph, a picture in sepia of a young woman—a girl, really—who gazed soberly into the distance. Her dark hair was worn loose and long, she had Paula's mouth, chin, and shape of face. *To Jim from Lorrie* was written on the back in ink faded to no-color. I looked at the book. Very small print. Small illustrations, pictures of Alice with hair worn loose and long. On the flyleaf a name was inscribed in youthful script. *Lorene Jessup.*

I replaced the photograph in the book, rewrapped the book and put it back in the drawer. Now what? Was it possible that Paula had put the money somewhere else and forgotten? Not likely, she was careful with money; three hundred dollars wasn't a royal ransom, but it wasn't fifty cents either. Also, there was this to say for compulsive neatness: if she said she put something somewhere, you could usually rely on it.

Just in case, I went to the bedside table on the other side, and checked. Not there either.

As I pondered, something caught my eye: a tiny fragment of broken glass sparkled up from the rug. I bent to retrieve it, then stared at what lay on my palm. Not glass. A sequin.

I turned and looked at the bed again, then back at my palm. He had been here last night. While I'd been dead to the world, out for the count, the two of them had been here together. At some point—perhaps while she was in the bathroom—he had snooped around, found the money, and helped himself. Or could I be doing him an injustice? Perhaps she had found the money, last night or earlier, and taken it. By her lights—*I'm their daughter, aren't I?*—there wouldn't be anything wrong with taking it. She wouldn't see it as stealing.

Still, I couldn't simply ignore what had happened, especially in view of Leo's call. I would have to put the question directly: *There was money in that drawer, Beth. Did you take it?* Either way, unless the money were returned, I'd have to let her parents know it was gone.

Meanwhile, what about tonight? I was sure she had gone back to Showplace. She would probably bring him back here again. If he had stolen once, he might steal again. But I could hardly stand in the door declaiming "He shall not pass!" Nor could I see myself frisking him as he left later. Anyway, I didn't even know for a fact that he was the guilty party. Should I wait up, make a point of being around when they arrived? Perhaps my presence would serve as deterrent or warning. Nonsense. Neither of them was likely to be so easily inhibited—by me, anyway. If Leo were here, or even Paula, it might be different. What to do? Round and round and round went the question.

• • •

At midnight, I was still wrestling with it. The party was still in full swing, I could still hear music, but I was no longer among the guests, dazzling one and all with my wit and sparkle. ("Who is that intriguing woman in blue? We must have her over.")

At one o'clock I turned off the light and lay down, fully dressed. Through the window came the strains of *In the Mood*, but the hubbub had lessened, things were drawing to a close. At one-thirty the music ended. There were sounds of cars driving away, people calling farewells. *Goodnight! Marvelous time! Perfectly wonderful! Tell Bibs I'll call!* Then silence.

By two o'clock I was half asleep. At two forty-five, I came abruptly awake at the sound of a car pulling up in the driveway. Followed by another. A car door slammed. Then another. Then came sounds of someone entering the house.

I stood in the dark at the top of the stairs. When they came upstairs, I'd stop them, question her—him/them. If she—he/they—admitted taking the money, I'd demand it back. If she—he/they—denied taking it, or refused to return it, I would at least have done all I could. The Tanners could hardly hold me responsible for the fact that their daughter was light-fingered, or that she brought questionable friends to the house.

I heard them now, coming up the stairs, speaking in undertones. By the time they reached the second floor, they were no longer talking.

*Now.*

I started down the stairs and encountered them just as they reached Paula's door. His arm was around her, his hand on her hip while she leaned into him. They halted abruptly when they saw me.

"Iris?" She looked puzzled, as though trying to remember who I was.

"Look who's here!" That wide loose smile. "Wanna join the party, Irene?"

Looking at Beth, at him, I felt appalled. How *could* she, with someone like this? "Beth. There was money, in the night table. Did you take it?"

Roy was suddenly alert.

She giggled. "Yeah. How'd you guess?"

"That's for household expenses—"

"That's me! Household expense!" She and Roy looked at each other, smiling.

"Beth, you know you shouldn't—"

"*Shouldn't!*" Her voice turned nasty. "Who're you to tell me what I shouldn't? Buzz off!" She waved a hand in dismissal.

"Beth—" I moved forward, took her arm. "Please—"

"You heard her, Reeney!" Roy gave me a push. "Shove off!"

The bedroom door closed sharply behind them.

My thoughts were in turmoil. I sank down on the stairs, trying to decide what to do. I could open that door, go in there and demand return of the money. But how far was I likely to get with *that?* I could threaten to call and tell her parents. That was likely to be equally effective. If it had been Roy who took the money, I could have demanded it back, threatened to call the police if he didn't give it back, but I couldn't do that with Beth.

Suppose I let it go for the moment, and made another attempt in the morning, after Roy had gone. She might be more amenable then, without him here egging her on. Yes. I'd bide my time till he left, then I'd ask for the money. If she wouldn't return it—well, she wouldn't, that's all. I'd have done all I could. But I would have to tell Leo, or Paula, or both, where the money had gone.

I went slowly upstairs and got into bed, feeling sick with apprehension. If only I hadn't begun to like her.

* * *

I didn't fall asleep for hours. When I finally did, I slept heavily and didn't wake until nine.

The house was silent. Still in my nightclothes, I went downstairs and stood outside that door, listening. Not a sound. They'd sleep till all hours, I guessed. Now what? While considering, I went back upstairs, dressed, made coffee in my kitchen, then carried a second cup downstairs and out to the deck.

A haze transfused the scene with a hint of mystery. Later the mist would burn away and every detail of this veritable Eden would stand revealed. An Eden now complete with serpent. I kept still, listening. Perhaps I'd hear voices from above, the way I'd heard Paula and Leo that time. But there were no voices, only stillness and the crying of gulls. They would probably sleep until noon at least.

Suddenly, an idea came: the second car I'd heard last night had been Roy's presumably—or, more accurately, Graham's. Was it possible Roy had already left? If so, I needn't delay any longer.

I hurried to check the driveway.

I was right: the wagon was there and the Porsche was in the garage, but Graham's car was nowhere to be seen. Roy had left.

I went and knocked at the bedroom door. "Beth! Are you awake, Beth?"

No answer.

"Beth?"

I opened the door.

The tumbled bed was empty. I went in, calling her name, as though she might be playing hide-and-seek. Pointlessly, I looked in the dressing room and bathroom. In the bedroom again, I stared around. The room looked different. The garments were gone from the chairs and doorknobs. It looked as though—no, surely not! I threw open the closet doors, looking for her suitcase. Gone.

Heart pounding, I ran downstairs.

A note lay on the kitchen table. My name was on it. It was scribbled on a sheet engraved P.T., torn from one of Paula's notepads.

*Taking off. I'll give a call sometime. Beth.*

My head spun, thoughts swirled formless as protoplasm. *We'll skip the highways, take the byways . . .*

I went to the telephone and dialed Graham's number.

"Graham—" I tried to sound casual. "Is Roy there, by any chance?"

"Roy's gone!" He sounded distraught. "Cleaned out the register, took the car! I can't believe it! I found a note— wait—" He read it to me. *"Moving on, Baxie. Thanks for everything. I'll take care of the old bus.* I can't believe he'd do such a thing!"

"I think Beth's gone with him, Graham. I found a note, too."

"So that's it! The little bitch! She was after him the minute she saw him, the cunt!" On and on he went, spewing out words I'd never heard him use. Could this be Graham, my gentle friend?

No, Graham, it was the other way around, I wanted to say. She was the next free ride, the next meal ticket. Or was I wrong? Was it she—? Oh, what difference did it make? They were gone. She was gone. That was what mattered.

"I thought of calling the police, reporting the car stolen. But that's no way to get him back. He'd hate me for it." His voice broke.

"Graham, let me know if you hear anything, will you? I'm concerned about Beth."

"About Beth?" He laughed. "Don't waste your time. A tough cookie, that one. She's been around. Nothing's going to happen to *her.*" He hung up.

A second later the telephone rang. I seized it.

"We're at LaGuardia, Iris." Leo's tone was brusque. "We'll be on the one o'clock flight. Is Beth there?"

"No." I swallowed. "As a matter of fact—"

"Never mind, we'll be there shortly. We ran into the Arnstroms, they'll give us a ride, you needn't meet us."

"All right, but—"

Too late, he'd rung off.

I stood as though paralyzed. Nothing I could do. Only one thing: get their room in shape.

Hurrying, I changed the linens, cleaned the bedroom, the bathroom, tidied, dusted, swept, scrubbed like someone possessed. As if this could change things. As if fresh sheets could eliminate the recent past and fend off the future. As if dust-free surfaces and a sparkling bathroom could push back the clock, replace that money, and bring Beth home.

# 11

LEO TOOK OFF HIS JACKET. Paula leafed through the mail. Something different about her. She looked wan, dispirited. In him, too, there was something different—a deeper reserve, like a barrier.

"What news from the home front?" Leo asked. "Where's Beth?"

Where indeed? Oh, God, how to tell them, how to explain? My heart raced. "Beth's gone," I said, in what I hoped was a non-alarmist tone.

"Gone?" Paula looked up. "When? Where?"

"This morning. I don't know where." I gave her the note. She read it aloud, her voice barely audible.

Leo's face darkened. "Here we go again." He looked at me sharply, as though I might be an accessory after the fact. "Did you know she was planning this?"

I shook my head. "She said nothing."

"Is she alone?" His eyes were on me.

"I don't know. I didn't see her leave."

He gave a nod, as though confirmed in his suspicions. "There's a man involved, no doubt. Unsavory, as usual. Well, let her go, if that's what she wants, she's not a child any longer. Don't worry, Paula, it's the same old story. We'll hear from her when she needs something."

I expected Paula to argue, but she didn't. She'd kept silent

*1 1 3*

all this while. The news simply didn't seem to register the way I'd expected.

"By the way—" He loosened his tie—"you did get that money?"

"I checked right after you called. It wasn't there."

"Wasn't there?" Paula's voice rose. "What do you mean, it wasn't there?"

"You know what she means, Paula. Beth took it."

"I don't know that! Neither do you! You're always willing to think the worst of Beth!" She turned to me. "Why didn't you take the money when I first told you about it?"

"You didn't say there was any urgency, and I didn't need it right then. Until your husband called, I'd forgotten it was there."

"I don't think you forgot! I think you took it!"

I stared in disbelief. Had she actually said that?

"That's disgraceful, Paula!" Leo's eyes flashed. "You owe Iris an apology!"

Paula covered her face with her hands. "Yes. I'm sorry." Her voice was muffled. "That was very bad. I can't think what came over me." Her hands dropped. "I have a headache, I'm going upstairs to lie down. Will you bring me an icepack, please?" She went out.

A ploy for sympathy to excuse her behavior? If so, she was out of luck. All she would get from me was ice. I opened the freezer door to get it, slammed it shut again.

Leo had followed me. "Iris, I'm sorry you were subjected to that." He strode out, heading towards his study.

Upstairs, Paula lay on the bed in her nightgown, an arm across her face. She hadn't bothered to remove the bedspread. That wasn't like her. "Would you get me some aspirin, please?" Not like her, either, that faint, quavery voice. As she struggled up to a sitting position, I was struck by the fact that she really did look unwell; her skin was pasty, her eyes looked small and sunken.

"Iris, will you forgive me? Please? I shouldn't have said it, I didn't really think it, not for—"

"It's all right," I said, curtly, in a way that would let her know it wasn't. Let her stew. "What shall I do about dinner?"

"I don't want any dinner. You'd better ask Leo what he wants, I suppose." She lay down again, holding the pack to her forehead.

Leo was at his desk. Files and papers were spread out everywhere. "Have we some boxes I can pack this in? I'm taking these back to the city tomorrow."

I said there were boxes in the storage area off the laundry room.

"By the way, what happened to the flower border? It looks as though a truck ran over it."

"Perhaps a delivery van misjudged."

His fingers twirled a pencil. I kept silent.

He cleared his throat. "I do hope you'll forgive Paula's behavior. She's going through a difficult time right now. In fact, I'm very glad you're here. It's good that she won't be alone when I leave. We—" He broke off.

In the ensuing silence we seemed to stand on the brink of a precipice which further words might take us over. His eyes met mine directly. All at once I felt uncomfortable, though exactly why I couldn't have said. Reaching for safety, I spoke in the uninflected tones of a servant. "Will you want dinner?"

He smiled faintly, as though he'd guessed my intention. "No, don't bother, thanks. I have to go into town on an errand, I'll get something there."

Indoors and out, a hush had fallen. Even the gulls seemed to have quieted. Yet all through the house, currents seemed to be humming beneath the silence.

Even up in my rooms, the atmosphere felt oppressive. Restless, I went down again and out to the deck, longing to get away. Could I take the wagon and go off for a while, just briefly? If I did, I ought to let her know; Leo had left a while ago for Staunton, she'd be alone if I went. I could knock on her door. But suppose she were sleeping?

While I tried to decide, the last of the daylight faded. There were still ten days till the end of August, yet suddenly it felt as though summer were over. Had something gone wrong with the natural order? Just now the tide was rolling in, the beach was nearly covered, the rocks were only partly visible. But perhaps something had happened to the tides, too. Perhaps the sea would keep coming in and never stop, perhaps the water would keep rising steadily until the rocks, the bluffs, the trees, this house, were all—

"Iris! Where are you, Iris? *Iris!*" Paula's voice was urgent.

"Out here." I flicked on the light.

Paula came out on the deck. She had put her kimono over her nightgown. Her hair fell in wisps around her face, which looked floury, as though she had powdered it with talc. "Where's Leo?"

"He went into town on an errand."

She sank down in a chair. "Iris, listen—" She leaned forward and spoke in a whisper. "Some things are missing. My jewelry—some pieces—*please don't misunderstand!* You're the only one I can ask!" Her eyes fixed on me with pleading. "My gold choker. My onyx and diamond pin. My emerald ring and—oh—" Her hands were clasped as though in anguish or entreaty. "Did you notice? Did she say anything that—"

"*Are you certain?*" I, too, was whispering. Two whisperers alone in that house, joined by knowledge. "Have you searched—"

"Did she use my room?"

"Yes." Do it the way they used to tell you to answer children's questions on sex: answer only the questions, add nothing extra.

"I ought to have put it away in the safe, but you were here, the house wasn't empty—"

I stiffened.

"Don't! I'm only trying to explain—to myself—why I— Did she wear—did you see—"

"Your choker, yes. And that silver bangle. Other things, at times. I didn't think anything of it. My daughter used to wear my things. It's not unusual—"

"But Beth has a history—" Her voice trailed off. "Whatever you do, don't tell Leo! He gets so angry with her, he might . . . do something extreme. Call the police or bring charges or—"

Round and round went the question—Beth or Roy? I could see Beth helping herself. *I'm her daughter, aren't I?* Equally clearly, I could see Roy, encouraged by the earlier find of cash, prowling in search of more. Or persuading Beth, euphoric with sex, drugs, who knew what, to find him more.

Just then there was the sound of a car.

"That's Leo. Say nothing!" she implored. Her hand gripped my wrist for a second; then, before I could speak, she had gone. I heard her going through the house.

"Leo?" she called.

From where I sat, I could hear his footsteps going up the stairs.

"Leo! Where were you?"

"I had to do an errand."

"You were calling her, weren't you?"

"I don't owe you any explanation, Paula."

"You owe me *something!*" It was almost a shriek. "After thirty-one years!"

"I've paid what I owe, many times over. You promised this wouldn't happen if I came."

"You promised you'd give me these two days!"

"You said you weren't feeling well enough to travel alone. I agreed to come with you since—"

"You agreed, yes. Couldn't wait for me to get out of town. Leave the scene clear for you and that—"

"It was your idea to come here, not mine. You could have stayed in the apartment."

"Stay where everyone knows, everyone's laughing?"

"No one's laughing, Paula. People couldn't care less one way or the other, if you want the truth."

"What would you know about truth, Leo?"

"That's enough, Paula. I'm leaving tomorrow."

"Tomorrow! You owe me tomorrow! You promised!"

"Paula, I'm going to sleep. I'd advise you to do the same."

A moment later, I heard the front door slam with such force that the deck shivered beneath my feet. A breeze rustled in the trees with a secretive sound, like the sound of Paula and me whispering. In the distance the hoot of a horned owl sounded mocking.

Ten minutes passed. Twenty. She didn't return. I kept thinking of that old song with saccharine melody, lyrics to match. *I'm putting all my eggs in one basket, I'm betting everything I've got on you.* Now all those eggs were smashed, wasted. Her own fault? Perhaps. But tonight she was carrying a double burden. I was the only one who knew.

*Good that she won't be alone.* Had my being here made it easier for him to take this step? Don't put that on me, Leo. *It would mean a great deal to me . . .*

Yes. Now I saw.

I checked the driveway. Both cars were still here. She couldn't be very far. Where first? The pool, then the bluffs. If not there, then—

But I found her right away, at the pool. She was sitting on the tile that bordered the pool, her feet in the water. Her hair was dishevelled. The hem of her nightgown dragged in the water. A relentless moon shone down, brightly etching each detail.

"Here you are." I kept my voice casual.

She raised her head. In that moment she was naked before me, stripped, exposed. If I blew so much as a single breath, she'd surely disintegrate.

"You heard," she said. It wasn't a question. She moved a foot, watching the water swirl around it. "He's going to marry her, he says. Six years younger than Beth."

"Come on." I stretched out a hand. "A night's rest will help." Feeble words, I knew. Others had used those words to me. "I'll fix you a drink or some warm milk. It'll help you sleep."

"I don't need sleep. I need—" Her voice faded.

"Yes. I understand."

The minute the words were out, I was sorry, even before I heard her laugh. If you could call it a laugh.

"You do, don't you? All along, you've been waiting for this—you and your understanding."

"Come on, Paula." I reached for her arm, bracing myself in case she pushed me. After a second, she yielded. Together, in the cruel moonlight, we walked back to the house.

# 12

SEPTEMBER. The houses around the cove were closed. The chairs on the porch of the Staunton Inn were mostly unoccupied—soon they'd be stored, though the Inn stayed open all year round. The maples had turned russet and gold, the open fields were gorgeous with fireweed. Shorebirds were on the move; on foggy nights they occasionally flew against lighthouses, attracted by the beam, and were killed.

Paula hadn't gone back to New York. She stayed in the house like a turtle withdrawn into its shell.

She wouldn't take the calls that came from the lawyer Leo had retained for his divorce; she wouldn't answer his letters; the pile of unopened envelopes mounted steadily higher.

He finally asked me to give her a message: since she wouldn't respond to any of his communications, would she give him the name of the lawyer who represented her?

No use. She hadn't engaged a lawyer. She didn't intend to. "This divorce talk is nonsense," she told me. "Give it time, this affair will wear itself out, like all the others."

Oh, she had known always, all these years. About all of them. "Inevitable for a man like that, well-known, attractive. Women have always made a play for him. Hard for him to resist."

She had understood, even accepted. "Though it had hurt, naturally." What she didn't accept, and wouldn't dignify by taking seriously, was this absurd talk of divorce and remarriage. To someone younger than his own daughter! Surely he knew how ridiculous he looked? "It's obvious what *she* wants, of course. Leo has money, connections, he can introduce her to the right people. If I were an actress just starting out, I'd pursue him, too."

On and on it went, day after day, a tape played endlessly, as though the words could keep reality at bay. She wanted no interjections of any kind from me, nor did I offer any. I was the last person to offer myself as a marital expert, even if she had wanted my opinion. "He always knew that I knew, though we didn't talk about it. I never made difficulties, never complained. I always felt that whatever he did, he wouldn't stray far, I had nothing to worry about . . ."

But gradually, as the days passed, the tape began to run down. Not that she changed her position—Leo was going to come back, no question. I had standing orders that if he called—when he called—I was to call her to the phone at once. But now, as though the energy that fuelled the recitation had run down, the monologue stopped. She grew quiet, hardly spoke—about anything. She no longer supervised the housework; I was left alone now to do the chores at my own pace, in my own way. Since she rarely went out of the house, I was delegated to get whatever she needed from Staunton, though she seldom expressed a wish for anything, except yarns for that everlasting crewel work that never seemed to get anywhere. Did she, like Penelope, unravel it at night, waiting for her man to return? She no longer swam, even when the weather permitted. She no longer played tennis. She no longer had her hair done. For the first time since I'd known her, her appearance became less than impeccable; her hair looked faded and stringy, she put on the same pants and sweater day after day, often she stayed in her nightclothes till afternoon.

I tried to get her to come along on errands. I suggested rides and walks. I scanned the local paper for attractions that might tempt her—a Cary Grant movie, Gilbert & Sullivan at the Unitarian Church, a day of Native American crafts and music, a talk on bird-banding (I was growing desperate). No use.

In the small hours, I'd hear sounds of nocturnal wanderings. I'd get out of bed and go find her, try to persuade her to go back to bed, but she wouldn't. I'd stay with her for a while, though she wouldn't talk. I got in the habit of keeping a deck of cards handy, and at two, three, four in the morning, we'd sit like characters in a silent film, playing lethargic gin.

One night this changed. As though someone had given a signal, pressed a button on one of those talking, walking dolls, she began to talk. Not about Leo, not about Beth, but herself. It was on these nights that I finally came to know Paula, came to know something about her earlier years with Leo, then further back, the years of her beginnings.

She told me about her mother, Lorene, Lorrie, eighteen when Paula was born. Dark-haired, pink-cheeked, with a dancing walk. The dancing walk took her right out the door one winter's day, for good. Paula was six months old. *I'm too young to have a baby, too young to be married and take care of a house,* she told her husband, who was sixteen years older, a feisty Irishman with ginger hair, a carpenter. Off she went one winter's evening, bag in one hand, skates in the other.

"Skates?" I asked.

"She loved ice-skating, he said. She used to skate whenever she could, as soon as the ponds froze over."

I saw a Victorian Christmas card, young woman with dark hair flying, hands in a muff, velvet skirt flaring as she glided along on the wintry ice, growing smaller, smaller, receding into the chilly distance, vanishing.

Her husband told no one at first. He hoped she'd come back. He let people think she had gone to visit her family in Ohio. He fitted out a toolbox with padding for Paula, put in a bottle and baby food, and took her along on his jobs. On his breaks, he'd feed her.

Like a slide show, this image succeeded the other. "He must have been quite a man."

"Yes," Paula said. "I see that now. It must have been hard for him. But later he began to drink. By the time I was in grade school, he wasn't working regularly. I'd come home from school and find him there. I used to dread coming home. He'd be rampaging around, or lying on the sofa, the floor, wherever. He'd be—" She stopped. "The place was always a mess, no matter how hard I tried."

There'd been a neighbor who was kind, took an interest, tried to talk to Paula's father. Betty Hartt was her name, a fat, motherly woman; her husband was the mail carrier. "I spent a lot of time in her house. I couldn't wait for the day when I'd get away from home. The only thing I had back then—well, I was pretty. Popular with boys. Being pretty, it seemed to me, was the only thing that got you what you wanted. When I was sixteen, I was going to run off with a boy I knew and get married. Betty Hartt heard about it, persuaded me to stay and finish high school."

Darkness pressed against the windows. A circle of radiance from the light above the kitchen table showed her face dragged down with the effort of memory. "So you see—" she gave a smile that mocked her words—"I've come a long way."

"What about Lorrie? Did you ever hear—?"

"Not from her, no. She died somewhere in the midwest years later, of cancer. They notified my father. I was twenty by then, gone to New York . . ."

I thought of the book wrapped in tissue, the sepia photograph. I thought of tapshoes on her seventh birthday. I thought of Betty Hartt, Elizabeth, Beth.

Outside this house my world seemed to be expanding as Paula's narrowed. I had started the computer course, to which

I drove with Lilly on Tuesday evenings. I had become friends with someone in the class, Ruth Pritchard, about my age and recently widowed. I was seeing someone else, too. A new element had entered my life. Three weeks after our disastrous outing, Jack Fielding had called. By then I'd begun to feel somewhat ashamed of my behavior. When he asked if we could try again, I was more than ready to meet him halfway. Did I care for chili? he asked. Good, it was his one culinary accomplishment. Would I come to dinner? I would.

It rained hard on the appointed evening. The heavens were always destined to open, it seemed, whenever I saw this man. At seven, I knocked at the door of the house he shared with three other people. A huge black and silver Harley-Davidson was parked in the driveway.

The man who opened the door was rather attractive, I thought, with that curly mouth and firm jaw. "I'm a friend of Jack Fielding's," I said, by way of introduction.

"Good. So am I." Why did he just stand there, grinning? Slowly, with disbelief, I realized. "You're not—!" Could one shave do all that? "You're beautiful!" I cried in best Hollywood fashion.

"Wait till I take my glasses off. You'll be overwhelmed!"

Why would a man who looked like this, with no absence of chin, weakness of mouth, or toady warts, hide himself in that fashion, I wondered, as he led me up to his quarters on the third floor. (We had that in common, I told him.) His room was spacious, spanning the entire length of the house. The furnishings were minimal but adequate—a long desk which could also serve for dining; sofa and easy chairs; bookshelves; stereo; oversized futon. Also a fireplace.

At the far end stood a black metal structure, which I studied while he fixed drinks. It was a tall, very thin figure, made of a single piece of metal. Tiny head at the top. "Did you make this?"

"Yes, that's what I do when I'm not making gates and railings to pay the rent." He came over and placed a glass in my hand. "That's yours truly, stretched to breaking point before I chucked things over and came up here. Come and be comfortable."

It turned out he'd been living in Merriam for nine years—six in this house. It took me aback. Nine years, even six, smacked of permanence. Did he intend to live like this always, I wondered? Shouldn't this kind of arrangement be a way station only, a pause on the way to something else? It seemed more appropriate to youth than to someone who, clean-shaven, was revealed as not too many years short of fifty.

This, too, we shared, I thought; we were both—inappropriate. Watching as he lit the fire, I could see why I'd thought him younger; that spareness went with youth, so did a certain laid-back quality. But now, looking carefully, I saw horizontal lines scoring the back of his neck, saw vertical lines down the sides of his face that hadn't shown beneath the beard. As he talked, he touched his naked chin from time to time, as though seeking the cover that had been there. My attention was caught by his hands, which were well shaped, with long fingers, though with dark cracks caused, I supposed, by his occupation.

I went with him down to the kitchen, where we collected the dinner he'd cooked before I'd arrived. A young woman with cropped red hair stopped in, carrying a motorcycle helmet. "Steve around?" she asked.

"I'm not sure. He's been in and out. Iris, this is Stacey Frye, one of my housemates."

"Hi. If you see Steve, tell him I could use a hand. My kickstart's acting up again."

Upstairs, flames leaped on the hearth and Satie's *Gymnopedie* played while we ate. Stacey was a reporter for the local paper, Jack said; on the side, she wrote mystery stories with a Down East background. Steve had a law degree but now built boats. Tina had a health food store and taught yoga.

And he?

"I used to do research for a pharmaceuticals firm, married the daughter of the man who headed the company. After Roz and I married, they whisked me out of the lab and made me VP. It didn't work out. I could have told them it wouldn't, if they'd thought to ask. Roz claimed I wasn't trying. She was right, to tell the truth. The whole thing had been a mistake. Things went downhill from there. The divorce was a relief for both of us. She married again not long after— a white-shoe guy. Better for her than I was, I guess. Good with the boys too, I gather." Tim, now twenty-two, had just graduated from Harvard and was going into physics. John was at Dartmouth. "They're both somewhat embarrassed by their old man . . ."

I thought, You, too?

*Gymnopedie* ended. He put on Big Joe Turner. *Oh, you're so beautiful, but you're gonna die some day! Oh, you're so beautiful, but you're gonna die some day! All I want's a little lovin' before you pass away . . .*

Need I say that not long after, we ended up, by natural progression, on that rock-hard futon? (He was devoted to it; it had cured his lower-back problem, he said.) As for me, I had no complaints at all. It was all so straightforward, pleasant, and remote up there, where no sounds from the house intruded, and the firelight played rosily on the walls and our nakedness.

My existence became schizophrenic. Outside the Tanners' house, I was enjoying life immensely. I went canoeing with Jack, I went hiking with the Wenzels, I picked huckleberries with Daphne and Alex. Then I'd come back to this place where Paula moved through the rooms like a restless ghost and the air seemed heavy with the pall of remembrance.

Tuesday evenings I'd get back late after going out to coffee with Lilly and others after class. Returning to the silent, darkened house, I'd find Paula sitting in front of the television.

"It's eleven o'clock," she'd say, fretfully. "It doesn't seem to bother you that I sit alone here."

"You don't have to, Paula. Go to the club, take in a movie, call someone."

Even as I said it, I felt guilty, for whom could she call? I felt torn between sympathy and impatience, but I wasn't going to sit and hold her hand. I had places to go and people to be with now whenever I was free. If she chose not to return to New York, so be it.

# 13

FOR SOME REASON I couldn't define, I hadn't told any of my friends that Paula and Leo had separated. Some instinct told me to keep these two aspects of my life as separate as possible. Graham was the only one who knew anything, and his knowledge was limited to Roy and Beth's departure.

At first, their disappearance had seemed to drive a wedge between us. Graham blamed Beth entirely, spoke of her in vituperative tones. To hear him tell it, Roy was an innocent she had led astray, a wide-eyed lad beguiled by a Jezebel.

"Nonsense," I said. "Roy's at least as culpable as Beth, if not more so."

"You don't know Roy the way I do," Graham assured me.

"And *you* don't know—" But then I stopped, for fear of what could not subsequently be unsaid. He must surely be aware of Roy's true character. Still, there was no point in rubbing his face in that knowledge. In any case, quarrelling with Graham wouldn't help Beth. On the contrary, through Graham I might get some word which I wasn't otherwise likely to hear. I kept thinking of those parents of the Sixties, forming clubs to seek news from each other of their runaway children.

"If I hadn't been at your house that night, the two of them would never have met. None of this would have happened."

"You mean it's *my* fault?" I said with asperity.

He had the grace to look ashamed. "I'm sorry. Of course not. It's just that I miss him so, you can't imagine."

"You don't seem to understand, Graham—I'm no happier about this than you are."

He gave me a commiserating look. "Is Madam dumping on you about it?"

"Paula? No. But I worry because—"

Because your golden boy has a psychopathic streak, not to mention an easy way with other people's property.

No, that last wasn't fair; I didn't know, might never know for certain, who had taken the jewelry. In any case, my worry about Beth and how she was faring at Roy's hands far exceeded worry about the jewelry. Only lately had I come to understand that I had grown much fonder of Beth than I'd realized. I sensed, too, that Beth had, to some extent, reciprocated that feeling. Would we all do better, I wonder, if we swapped our offspring for other people's when they reached their teens, and switched back again five or ten years later?

Ultimately, Graham went out and bought the cheapest second-hand car he could find, so disreputable-looking that he kept it parked behind his shop. He couldn't afford anything better right now. "Anyway," he said, wistfully, "Roy may be back. Then I'd have two, wouldn't I?"

Finally, nearly two months after their departure, there was news, of a sort. But it didn't come from Graham.

I'd been out with Jack, and came home from his place around three in the morning. He always protested my leaving in the middle of the night, but I felt uneasy about Paula's being alone in the small hours.

Now, as I let myself into the silent house, Paula was on me like a fury. "*Where were you?* I called everywhere, those people, the Johnsons—Oh!" She pressed her hands to her temples. Her voice ran on, babbling, almost incoherent.

Suddenly what she was saying came through.

"*Beth called?* When?"

"At eleven. I've been waiting and waiting—"

"Where is she?"

"London."

"*London?* What's—"

"I don't know. I couldn't really understand her properly. You know how she gets sometimes. She kept going on and on about music. Checking out the music scene, she said. Dancing, does she mean?"

To his tune, no doubt.

"I asked her to come back. She said she didn't have the fare. I told her I'd wire a ticket."

"Then what?"

"She hung up—without saying where to send it."

Her mouth worked. She looked suddenly elderly. Even her posture had changed lately; she, who had always been so rigidly upright, now looked almost stooped.

"She'll call again, Paula."

Would she, though, I wondered privately. Could Leo find her, perhaps? Through the embassy or his connections? Might she have called Leo, in fact?

I said, "Perhaps we should get in touch with your—with Leo—"

"No! He'd call the police to trace her. He's done that before. She'd misunderstand, run away."

Because of the jewelry, she meant. She might be right. "Still, Paula, you should feel better, now that she's called."

"Should I?" She gave me a strangely hostile look. "It was you she really wanted to talk to."

"Paula—"

"The call was person to person. To you. When I told the operator you weren't here and I didn't know where to get in touch, she finally said she'd talk to me."

She went back to her room and closed the door.

• • •

Beth didn't call back. Paula now stopped eating almost entirely. She almost never bothered to get dressed. She spent nearly all the time in her room, with the TV going, bent over her needlework.

Watching, I thought of wimpled medieval women seated at their embroidery hoops, bosoms rising and falling as they plied their needles, while their men rode gloriously off to conquer, sack, pillage, and rape. Whatever did they do with all that embroidery? No matter, it kept them occupied, had a certain calming effect, I suppose, probably saved them—in some cases—from total madness. But it didn't seem to be helping Paula.

Finally, something happened which propelled me into action.

The station wagon had developed a problem; it ran, but it kept stalling. I told Paula I thought I should take it to Probert's and have them check it. She was in her room watching, of all things, a talk show dealing with May-December marriages. At noon on this sunny autumnal day, she lay on her bed in nightclothes, with a blanket over her legs like an invalid.

At first, she didn't answer.

"Paula, did you hear what I said?"

She spoke absently, eyes on the screen. "Let it go till Leo comes. He'll fix it."

Had she really said that?

I said, carefully, "I don't think we should let it go till then."

"Oh, all right, take it in if you really think it can't wait."

I took the car to Probert's that afternoon. It needed only a minor adjustment. They could get it done in half an hour.

While they worked on the car, I went to a nearby drugstore and called Leo's office.

"Who's calling, please?"

I gave my name. While I waited for him to come on the

line, a thought occurred to me: what if he asked if we'd heard from Beth? Should I tell him? Or should I follow Paula's wishes? Paula didn't make much sense these days, but about this her instincts were probably right. All right, I'd lie, if necessary. It would be easier to lie over the phone, without those eyes boring into me.

Still, I felt a slight quiver of uneasiness as I heard his voice. "What's up, Iris?"

He sounded briskly welcoming—but also slightly wary. I told him.

"I'm really worried. I think she's in a serious state."

"Iris, I'm sorry, but I'm the last person—"

"Who else is there? This isn't *my* responsibility."

"Of course not. But I don't see how I can help."

"Would you consider making a brief visit here, to talk to her? Perhaps she'd respond—"

"It's out of the question. What good would it do? The only thing she wants to hear is that I'm coming back. My coming would only make things worse. She'd deliberately misinterpret."

He was probably right. "But we can't simply ignore what's happening," I insisted.

Silence.

"There's a mental health centre near Tiscat. Could you get her to go to a therapist there?"

"I can't even get her to go for a walk!"

"It's worth a try. If she'll listen to anyone, she'll listen to you. I know you have your hands full, Iris. As of now, I'm doubling your salary."

"But—"

"I'm afraid I have to go now, there's a conference waiting."

The resentment sparked by his words increased with every mile as I drove back to the house. Despite the way he'd manipulated me in the past, and a certain sympathy I felt for Paula, I could nevertheless understand why he'd left. I could even sympathize—who better?—with his bid for another chance, a different partner. But how could he so quickly and completely disconnect from his former life? Did he feel no responsibility at all towards Paula?

Apparently not. The offer of a doubled salary was supposed to take him off the hook, obviously. This was to be my reward for assuming the responsibility he'd abdicated. He thought that took care of it, did he? The more I thought about it, the angrier I grew. Make your mess and run away, leaving the maid to clean it up—a pat on the head and some extra cash will take care of it.

And Beth—what about Beth? I'd worried about how I'd answer when he asked about her, but he hadn't even thought to inquire. Had he completely given up on his daughter? Once again I seemed to hear Beth's voice, desolate, *Life is just a bowl of crud.* Had he ever taken the trouble to sit down and talk to her? Had he ever tried to find out what the problem might be?

Come on, be fair, he's probably tried over and over. Anyway, how successful have *you* been in your relationship with Callie? He would probably have better luck with Callie, I thought ruefully—as I might have done better with Beth, given longer acquaintance. Though if what I heard was true, he wouldn't waste time talking to Callie, he'd whip her into bed quick as a wink.

Back at the house, Paula had transformed day into night; the shades in her room were drawn, the lamps were lit, the television was running at high volume.

I marched to the window and let up the shades. She cringed as the room was flooded with daylight.

"Why do you do this, Paula?"

"You were gone. The house seems so big and empty—"

"Don't stay in the house! Take a drive, go for a walk, come with me and do some shopping!"

She turned her head away, silent.

I flung up my arms. "I give up!" I started for the door.
"Where are you going?"
"Who knows? I'm certainly not hanging around here. Plenty
of things I'd rather do."
"But you've just come back," she almost wailed.
"So? I've finished my work for the day."
"You're always leaving me—"
"Come with me, then. We'll go for a walk."
She didn't move.
"Well? I warn you, I'm not staying in here on a day like
this."
I waited.
Slowly, reluctantly, she got off the bed.

We tramped along the bluff together.
It had turned colder despite the brightness; a cutting wind
had blown up.
She shivered. "I'm freezing."
"Move faster." I sounded like a marine sergeant, but gentler
tones hadn't prevailed. "Look at the ocean, how wild and
lovely."
She turned her head away, shuddering. "I don't like it."
All at once, pity moved me. I halted. "Paula—" I took
her hand—"this can't go on."
"What?"
"You know. You need professional help, someone to talk
to."
She said, defiantly, "If I want to talk, I'll talk to you."
"That isn't the same."
"I don't care!" She pulled her hand away. "Don't try to
give me orders!" A flash of her former arrogance.
I took hope. It seemed healthier than what had been
happening lately.

# 14

TWO DAYS LATER, she came out with me and Ruth Pritchard
for an evening.

I told Ruth just enough to explain why I was bringing
Paula along. "She and her husband have separated. It's a
difficult time, she's feeling low. It'll do her good to get out
and see another face."

"Of course."

Ruth was warmly understanding, as I'd known she would
be. She knew what it was like to find yourself suddenly
alone. She'd moved here from Boston five years before, when
her husband had taken a job teaching political science at the
university. Then, six months ago, Bob had died of a heart
attack. She wasn't sure yet what her next step would be.
Her son was in graduate school. She might go back to teaching
English or she might not. She might go back to Boston where
she still had friends and some family.

"It's so beautiful here, Ruth. Wouldn't you miss it?"

"I'll keep the house for summers. But you haven't been
through a winter here. It gets pretty bleak."

That evening seemed a breakthrough for Paula. For the
first time in weeks, she put on make-up and got dressed in
a good skirt and sweater, suede jacket, silk scarf.

"My hair looks dreadful."

"It'll do for tonight. Why don't you get it done soon?"

Ruth turned out to be exactly the right person for this maiden voyage. She asked no questions, kept away from sensitive subjects, and chatted easily about herself and matters which were in no way threatening. She had found a gorgeous sweater at Brayer's, handmade, warm as a blanket. Her son, in his first year of medical school, had lately developed an interest in, of all things, jazz violin, and was taking lessons. Something had gone wrong with her furnace; the people she'd called couldn't seem to fix it.

Here, Paula came out of semi-silence to suggest a name. "He's very good, and reliable. Always turns up when he says he will. Not many do." She sounded, just then, like the old Paula.

The movie, too, was just right: *Mr. Smith goes to Washington.* Nothing heavy, nothing sad, nothing to remind anyone of recent changes, personal losses.

As Paula and I drove home later, Paula broke the silence. "When did he die? Ruth's husband?"

"Six months ago."

"Were they happy?"

"Reasonably so, I gather."

"Better to have him die than leave."

"Paula, that's—!" I was shocked.

Then I realized that, in an awful kind of way, this denoted progress: it was acknowledgement, finally, of the fact that Leo had gone.

After that there was no more talk about Leo's return. What I heard instead was something else: in all this time, I hadn't heard her weep, but now, over the next few days, she wept. It was as though, for the first time, reality had hit her. She was grieving now, yes, but it was a step forward; after this she could go on to the next stage, face up to the future, take hold.

From then on, she seemed to get better. With just a little urging from me, she now got out of bed at a reasonable hour and got dressed right away. She began to leave the house, to do errands, to shop—with me, and alone. When I asked her one day about a local history museum I'd heard of on one of the islands, she said she had never seen it, but she'd like to, and suggested we go there the following day for an outing.

Next day we drove to the dock and took the ferry over to Buford on Dart Island. Buford, with its shade trees, cottages, and spired churches, looked totally untouched by commerce. The museum turned out to be closed, so we headed for the rocky beach with its panoramic view of the open Atlantic. We walked along the top of Hale Beach and discovered sections of old stone fences left over from the days of sheep pastures and hayfields and apple orchards. We explored an old cemetery, where most of the names on the lichen-covered stones seemed to be from one family. We found our way to Tipping Cove.

That day we were together longer than we had ever been outside the house. She became more open and at ease than I had ever known her. What I remembered, as I looked back later, was that we laughed a great deal. She talked about people in the town where she'd grown up. Eccentrics. A steady churchgoer who arrived every fourth Sunday entirely in the buff. A woman who kept her house filled with parrots, all trained to talk; the minute a stranger walked in, the place turned to bedlam. A man who wrote passionate love letters in purple ink to people seriously ill in the hospital. She talked, too, about people she'd known when she'd first gone to New York. "Before Leo," she said, and for a second grew quiet, but then it passed and she went on talking. About the friend she'd first roomed with, who'd ended up marrying an Indian potentate. About modeling one of the world's most famous diamonds. About a cruise to the Caribbean on the yacht of a millionaire newspaper owner.

She told me something that surprised me. "There was a time I could have gone into business. When I was first married, I still did some modeling, just enough to keep my hand in. Leo said he'd finance me if I wanted to start an agency of my own."

"You didn't want to?"

"Not back then. I think I saw myself going on forever in those days, saw everything going along just as it was. Perfect, it seemed to me. I felt so lucky to have a man like that who loved me. I didn't want to do anything except be married, be Leo's wife. I kept thinking that way for a long time. Even when things began to change, I didn't realize at first. I couldn't see it." She shrugged. "A pity, in a way. I'm not clever or artistic, like Leo and his friends, but I might have been a good businesswoman."

She still could be, I said. It didn't have to be a modeling agency. It didn't have to be in New York. "With money, you can go anywhere, make a fresh start."

"At my age?" She shook her head. "I'm almost sixty."

I think we both enjoyed that day. I know I did. We were like two women who've known each other for years, been good friends for a long time. I had never seen her like this before, with her nervousness, defensiveness, pretensions stripped away. Not with me, certainly, nor with any of the people who'd been at the house over the summer. Not even, I suddenly realized, with Leo. Perhaps—only gradually did this come to me—she had never really been comfortable with Leo or with the people she had known through him. Years ago, while she had still been young and exquisite, and Leo's adoration had still wrapped around her like a blessing, it would have been easier. But after that she must have begun to feel dull, small, insignificant as a fly on the wall, in that high-powered company. And straining, always, in the effort to keep up, or to appear to be keeping up. It must have been like my holding on to those jobs by the skin of my teeth, barely making it, always knowing I wasn't really qualified. Oh, everyone would always have been polite, courteous, amiable, but their real feelings would have come through. She'd have felt it; she wasn't insensitive, wasn't blind, though she'd pretended blindness for a long time, about one thing and another. I saw it now: what she had always regarded as her great good fortune had really been her undoing.

In their early years, Leo must have known *this* Paula, the one I was seeing now, who was easy to be with, sensible, natural. Exquisitely beautiful too, back then, and so ready to love—even idolize—a man she could respect, after life with her father. Her very simplicity, her uncomplicated psychic needs compared to the people he knew with their vast though necessary egos and demanding temperaments, must have been a distinct relief to him at first. Before he began to grow bored and look elsewhere, and she began to grow frantic.

We took the ferry back again, got in the car and started the drive home.

"Let's stop at Driscoll's for dinner."

"I can't, Paula. I have class tonight."

"Can't you skip it, for once?"

"I can't."

She turned sullen. Suddenly I saw Beth when I'd turned down the wine.

Beth. What had happened to Beth? There'd been no further word. Hardly a day went by without Paula mentioning her in some way—not the present Beth but Beth as a child, as though talk of those simpler times might displace the difficult present. Seeing a TV interview with a children's author, Paula would tell me about the *Madeline* books Beth had loved. "I had to read them to her over and over. I can still remember . . . *In an old house in Paris that was covered with vines, Lived twelve little girls in two straight lines* . . ." Today we'd passed a boy riding a horse, and she'd talked about a pony Beth had owned. Still looking after the rider, she'd said, in a voice of longing, "If only she'd call."

"She will, Paula. I'm sure she will."

"I don't care what she took, doesn't she know that? I just wish she'd come home, let me try to help her."

"She will, Paula. Give it time."

Please let it be true. It must be. It would be. This wasn't her first such jaunt, after all. Roy was just one in a sleazy procession. But Roy—no, don't think of that. Think about Beth, a natural survivor.

"Computers!" she said now, in a voice of scorn. "Why on earth would you bother with something like that?"

In my head a light flashed *caution.* "It's just something I thought might be fun."

Actually I was finding it fascinating. To my surprise I had discovered an aptitude for this miracle of modern technology. I was always the first one in class ready to go to the next step. "That's the ticket! Coming on like gangbusters!" my instructor said.

But now I kept my tone careless. "It's just a short course, the most rudimentary fundamentals."

Paula finally went to the hairdresser. So did I. My going was her idea. She had taken hold of my hair, her touch knowing, professional, as she bunched it up, let it fall. "If you wore it just a little shorter, it would be bouncier, fuller. I think it would suit you. Come and let Maurice fix it."

So I did. And was pleased with the result.

"That really is very attractive, Iris."

"Thanks. So's yours. I like that middle part for a change."

She looked better just then than she had for ages. Failing a visit to a therapist, a visit to the hairdresser was surely the next best thing. Perhaps even better. By now, I'd stopped pushing her about a therapist. One could push only so far. Therapy wouldn't be effective in any case, unless she were receptive. Anyway, she seemed to be on the right road now.

From Maurice's, we went shopping. "Look." She pointed

to a poster tacked on the wall. *Harborside Orchestra. "Pops" at the Firehall.* "Let's go tonight."

"I'm sorry, Paula. I'm busy."

"Oh? Class again?"

"No. I'm seeing a friend."

"Is it important?"

"To me, yes."

"You make it sound like a heavy date." Her tone was ironic.

I said, firmly, "It is," and left the room to end it.

I don't know why that particular incident seemed to make a difference. I'd been going to other places without her. Perhaps it was just that the evening with Ruth, our expedition to Dart Island, our joint visit to the hairdresser, had set up certain expectations. By now she was taking it for granted that I'd be available whenever she wanted.

Before I left the house that evening to meet Jack, I put my head around the door of her study. "There's veal from yesterday for dinner, Paula."

"Are you going to have dinner?"

"Not here, no, but—"

"I don't think I want any, then. By the way, what time—"

"What?"

"Nothing." She smiled at me. "Have a lovely evening."

Delightful, to be wearing a dress, to have been to the hairdresser, to come into a restaurant and see a personable man waiting for you, watch his face light up as he sees you.

"You're looking pretty spiffy, if I may say so. Ravishing, in fact, if you'll pardon me for being fulsome."

Over dinner he told me he had a surprise.

"Tell me."

"When we leave."

When we left, there it was, in shining splendor in the

parking lot—a brand-new car. The first car he'd bought since he'd lived here.

"All your fault. I'm becoming much too effete."

"You'll find it's handy for keeping the rain off," I said, as we drove away.

"And making out."

"Yes, that's not so easy on a bicycle."

Much later, back at his place, I got ready to leave.

"It's just past twelve-thirty!"

"Even so."

"Goddamit, you're not indentured!"

I pulled my dress on over my head. "She was in sort of a funny mood."

"So am I. I have this perverted desire to keep you here."

I blew him a kiss. "I'll be back for a return engagement, I promise."

Yet when I got back and found the house in darkness, and no light coming from under her door, I regretted that I'd hurried back. Jack was right, I thought.

Next morning another surprise awaited me. Paula stopped me as I started out to the deck with shammy and cleaner. "Leave it. Someone's coming from the village in future to do windows and floors."

I hardly knew what to think as I retired my shammy. Was this promotion? Or what?

# 15

OUT OF THE BLUE, when I'd given up expecting it, Callie called.

I hadn't heard from her since I'd written her and sent a first check towards what I owed her, followed by a second check and then, out of my recently increased salary, the balance. I had really hoped—expected—that she would answer my letter, acknowledge the checks as a sign that she recognized I was doing better. When she hadn't done so, I'd been disappointed, but some obstinate pride had kept me from calling. Her turn, I told myself. Anyway, I didn't want to seem to be pushing her, bothering her. Heaven forbid I should bother her.

But now, hearing her voice, a rush of gladness swept over me. "Good to hear from you, Callie."

She said, rather stiffly, "I'm sorry. I did get your letter. And the checks, thank you. It's just—I seem to be swamped lately."

"How are you?"

"Oh . . . fine."

But she didn't sound fine, I realized suddenly. "Is something wrong?"

"No, no." But her voice kept that hollow ring. "The thing is, I'm coming east soon. If it's convenient for you, I thought perhaps I'd pay you a visit."

"Wonderful! When?"

"October fifth. Short notice, I know. Would you be able to get out? Do you—get time off?"

For good behavior? "Of course. I can put you up, too. I've a sofa bed in my living room. Is it a business trip?"

"No." Why did she sound so constrained? "You haven't heard?"

"Heard what?" My heart thumped. What was wrong? Was she ill? Was—

"Daddy's getting married."

Ah. So here we had it. Now I understood. For Callie, on whom Harry had concentrated so intensely, this would be a definite shock, even though Harry had been single for a while and Callie had gone off to a life of her own.

"Mother? I'm sorry, I guess I shouldn't have broken it so suddenly. Are you upset?"

I hesitated, probing myself cautiously for pain, the way Harry might probe a patient. No, I'd felt a slight jolt just now when I heard, but that was all. I no longer felt any emotional ties to Harry.

"No, Callie, I'm not upset. Are you?"

"Oh—not really. Just that—well, it's a surprise, that's all."

"They've been living together for some time, haven't they?"

"No. They only met two months ago."

It wasn't Swiss Miss, then. "Who is she?"

"A pediatrician. Wendy Robbins. They met at a colloquium in Kansas City."

"What's she like?"

"Don't know. I've only seen her picture. She's been married before, has a seven-year-old son, Alistair."

Hmm. How would Alistair make out with Harry, I wondered. And vice versa.

"I guess it's good that they have medicine in common," she said. How forlorn she sounded. "They're having a civil ceremony. The Gurnseys are giving a dinner reception."

The Gurnseys? Muriel and Tom, once my friends, were giving them a dinner? Somehow, that bothered me more than the idea of the marriage. Did everyone have these little hidden pockets of vulnerability, not acknowledged, not even suspected, until particular circumstances brought them to light?

"I told Daddy at first I wouldn't be able to get away, but he kept after me. I guess he really wants me to be there."

"Will you be coming here before or after?"

"After. You're sure that's all right?"

"Absolutely. It'll be so good to see you, Callie. Let me know what flight. I'll meet you. This call will cost you a fortune—"

"Never mind. Which reminds me, there wasn't any rush about that money. Are you all right now? Financially? Because if not—"

"I'm fine, thank you, not short of a thing." How satisfying, to be able to say it.

"You sound . . . different."

"Yes. Things are working out, Callie."

All at once our positions seemed reversed; she was the one in need of comfort.

"I understand how you feel, Callie, about your father. It's going to be all right, though. You'll feel better about it as time goes by."

Could I be certain? Probably not. But there were times, surely, to put forth positive statements in a tone of confidence, no matter how less than completely confident one actually felt. No matter how much I wanted to, there was no way to protect Callie from all the events and conditions of life that might hurt her. I would have to get used to that, learn to accept it. So must she. Meanwhile, this much I could offer—understanding, a listening ear, and a note of reassurance for the future.

Afterwards, replaying our conversation, Callie's and mine, I found nothing that, given another chance, I would hold back or add—nothing, for once, that made me feel lacking or guilty. For the first time, I felt some hope about my chances with Callie. Perhaps, on this visit, she and I would somehow find our way back to each other.

Paula was delighted to hear Callie would be coming.

"I'm so glad for you, Iris! We'll put her in the room down the hall."

She meant the one Vivian had used, with its own deck and view of the sea.

"Paula, there's no need. Really. Callie will sleep in my bed and I'll use the sofa bed in my living room."

She wouldn't hear of it. I must make up the guest room with the best linens. She herself put French soap in the bathroom and a stack of the latest magazines on the night table.

"Does she like to read in bed? If so, let's give her the other lamp—"

"This one's perfectly all right, Paula. Everything's lovely, couldn't be better."

"I want her to feel comfortable."

"Of course. So nice of you, Paula."

Inwardly, I was beginning to feel slightly aggrieved. She meant well, of course, but I resented the way she seemed to be taking over. Callie would be wrapped in total luxury down here, but I'd have preferred her to be upstairs with me. To what extent would I now have her to myself? We had so much time to make up for.

When I first glimpsed Callie at the airport, I hardly knew her. Her hair was now short and wavy; it showed off her delicate neck and pretty ears. Her face was skillfully made up in a way that brought out her eyes and the shape of her cheekbones. But I wished, just for a second, for the former Callie. I didn't know this Callie. This was an older, more sophisticated woman than the daughter I remembered. Not that she wasn't lovely. How collected and self-possessed she seemed. Watching her, in that second before she saw me, I saw how she must look to her colleagues and clients, to people who had never known the younger Callie, who couldn't ever see the image I held and perhaps would always hold, to some extent, as parents do.

On Callie's face, as she first caught sight of me, I saw a look of apprehension, almost distrust, before she made a split-second adjustment. Smiling now, she hurried towards me. As we met, she leaned slightly forward and kissed me. No embrace. "You're looking very well," she said, with a hint of surprise.

"So are you!"

We were both laughing a little, with nervousness, I think.

"You've cut your hair, Callie."

"Yours is different, too."

I took her hands. "How are you?"

"All right. The wedding wasn't as difficult as I thought it would be. And you?"

"I'm fine," I said, cheerfully.

"Yes. You seem—on top of things." She sounded relieved, and again—unmistakably—surprised.

Back at the house, Paula swept forward to greet her. "Welcome! I've heard so much about you, Callie. I may call you Callie, mayn't I?"

"Of course. Very kind of you to put me up. What a beautiful house."

Paula dipped her head graciously. "Let me know if there's anything you need. Iris, a call came for you. From—Mr. Baxter, is it? Call him back when you've time."

She retired, leaving us alone. I led Callie up to the bedroom, where I couldn't help smiling at her expression. "Think you'll be able to manage in here? Come see the view."

We stood on her deck and looked out over all the wonders that nature had to offer.

Then I showed her my quarters. She admired everything,

remarked how comfortable and convenient it all seemed, everything self-contained.

"I thought you said I'd be staying up here with you?"

"Paula thought you'd be more comfortable down there, with more room to spread out. And there's no deck up here."

"I don't care about the deck. I'd rather have been up here, close by."

My heart warmed to hear her say it.

"Never mind, it's only for one night, anyway. You'll be comfortable and private down there. We'll be together the rest of the time."

After she'd seen the rest of the house, we went down to the beach. "Well?" I asked, as we strolled along. "What do you think?"

"Of what?"

I made a broad gesture, encompassing the scene.

"Beautiful," she said, then paused. "Your situation here isn't quite what I'd pictured."

"You mean, no attic room, no frilly cap, no yes-Madam, no-Madam, right-away-Madam?"

I meant it as a joke, was laughing as I spoke, but her lips tightened, her expression turned sour. What was the trouble *now*, for God's sake?

She gave a forced smile. "I must say, she seems quite charming. How do you get along?"

"We didn't, at first. Not at all. But we do quite well nowadays, all things considered."

Back at the house, I sat on Callie's bed while she unpacked and changed into pants.

"Here you are." She handed me a small package. "Hope you like."

Inside was a pendant on a silver chain, a carved ivory figure two inches tall, rather primitive.

"Beautiful, Callie!"

"I remember you liked ivory, didn't you?" She leaned

forward to the mirror as she applied lipstick. "Actually, it's a fertility symbol."

"*What?*" I took another look.

"You wouldn't really notice, would you? Unless someone drew your attention."

"What a gift for your old mother. I'm highly flattered!" Wait till I showed it to Jack. A pity none of my friends would meet Callie. I would have loved to show her off, but had decided against it. More important for us to have this brief time to ourselves. And already it was three o'clock, most of the day was gone. She was taking the nine o'clock flight the next morning.

At five-thirty, we were up in my rooms when Paula's voice came crackling from the intercom. "Iris, I'd like you and Callie to come down for a drink."

I hesitated. I didn't want to hurt her feelings. On the other hand, Callie and I were just getting nicely settled, just beginning to talk about some things that were important. Oh well, we'd be alone for dinner. I had made a reservation at Taber's.

"It sounds lovely, Paula. We'll be right down."

Paula had put herself out. There were not only drinks but hors d'oeuvres which she had made herself. She conversed pleasantly, asking Callie about her work, and San Francisco. San Francisco was wonderful, wasn't it, all those cultural attractions. Did she know Polly James, by any chance? Polly ran a wonderful little seafood restaurant, Scales, in Sausalito. She and Polly had once worked together, years and years ago . . .

There we sat, in the vast white reaches of the living room, Paula talking away, handing around crab canapés, jumping up to get refills. When I stood to help, she waved me down. "I'll take care of it, Iris."

It was too much, she was overdoing, trying too hard. It

made me feel uncomfortable, self-conscious. Surely Callie felt it, too? I glanced surreptitiously at my watch. Six-thirty.

Yes, Callie said, San Francisco was beautiful and offered a great deal—opera, galleries, that marvelous museum. She hadn't been to Scales, but friends had been there and reported favorably. Yes, quite a large firm, twenty-four partners and thirty-nine associates, of which she was one. Five floors in the McAdam Building.

Six forty-five.

I stood. "Paula, this has been so nice, but we have to be getting along."

"Where are you going?"

"To dinner. I've—"

"But I have a surprise!" she announced, gaily. "I've booked for us at the club!"

"That's very generous of you, Paula, but—"

"Not at all, it gives me the greatest pleasure! Quite all right to go in pants," she said briskly to Callie, then picked up the empty glasses and hurried off to the kitchen.

I followed. "Paula, I've made a reservation at Taber's."

"Far better food at the club, you know. Now, Iris—" She turned, smiling—"please don't make an issue of this. You know I wouldn't do it if I didn't want to."

Dinner was splendid, of course. I resented every minute of it, at first. Then I chided myself, told myself to accept it graciously, take it as it was intended. This certainly was a prettier setting than Taber's. *And* better food, as she'd said. If it had been just Callie and me, it would have been perfect.

Don't be small, I told myself. She's been so good about everything. That room for Callie. And the way she welcomed her, and cocktails, and now—

Goddamit, did she have to come along?

By the time dinner was over, it was all I could do to thank her with a semblance of gratitude. Callie did it well, sounding delighted and grateful. Callie had obviously acquired superb social graces along with her new appearance.

Paula noticed nothing, clearly. She seemed very pleased with herself and the evening. Back at the house she bade us goodnight. "I'm going to turn in. You'll be sure to get all the lights, Iris, when you're through?"

Callie and I went upstairs a few minutes later, and settled down in my living room.

"I'm sorry we got stuck with that, Callie."

"Stuck?"

"I mean, with her. But she meant well. Under the circumstances, I couldn't really—"

"But everything was lovely," Callie said. "And she was perfectly fine, I thought. She's really very nice."

I studied her, sitting across from me on the sofa. Did she mean it? Or was she trying to make me feel better?

"What's her husband like? He's in New York, I suppose?"

"Yes. They've separated."

"Oh?" She sat forward abruptly, frowning. I could see wheels going round. "What's this going to do to *you*?"

"To me?"

"What are her plans? Will they keep this house? She isn't going to stay here, is she? Or is she?"

"I don't know, Callie. It's recent, this development. She'll go back to New York ultimately, I imagine."

"Then what?" She sounded alarmed. "What will you do?"

"I haven't yet thought—"

"But you have to! You have to look out for yourself! That's been the trouble all along—you don't think beyond the next five minutes!"

"Callie—" I was beginning to get annoyed.

"You breeze along as though some guardian angel's going to take care of you! There's no such thing. *You* have to do it!"

"Callie, I know that!"

"Do you? You act like a kid playing some kind of game—

never mind the future, never mind making a serious effort!"
She jumped up, agitated. "Do you seriously think you can
be a maid for the rest of your life? Pardon me—*housekeeper!*
You must have been crazy to take this kind of job in the
first place—Joanna thought so, everyone thought so, but you
wouldn't listen!"

"That's enough, Callie!" I was really angry.

"No, it's not! Nothing's enough! *Nothing gets through to
you!*" She stood over me now. "I'm worried sick, don't you
know that? I'm frightened! I can't think what'll happen if
you don't get your life straightened out. I can't bear it!" She
turned away with a kind of strangled sob.

My anger dissolved. My heart seemed to turn over, with
love, sadness, contrition.

From beyond the windows came the thin tolling of a bell
buoy. A branch tapped lightly at the window.

I put my arms around Callie as she wept. I talked quietly,
told her she needn't worry any more, it was going to be all
right. "Trust me, Callie. I understand what you're saying."
I put a tissue in her hand and she wiped her eyes.

Things had changed, I told her. *I* had changed, though I
couldn't offer hard evidence yet. "At the right time, Callie,
I'll make my move." I paused. "I don't think you realize,
I'm not—collapsed any more."

She looked at me, warily assessing.

"When the right time comes, I'll know what to do. And
I'll be ready for it."

I hadn't known that was true until I heard myself say it.

In fact, though I didn't say so to Callie, I had already
begun, in a cursory way, to glance through the want ads.
Marcus was right, there wouldn't be much around here, but
there was no harm checking.

I'd been thinking a lot about Marcus's offer lately. Or
rather, about my reaction to it. Six months ago I'd have
leaped at that offer, taken the money without a second's
hesitation. No more. There'd be no more freeloading unless

I were desperate. But I wasn't desperate. I had a feeling I wasn't going to be, either, no matter what the future might hold.

Was this new confidence simply due to the passage of time inevitably dimming memories of failure? Or was it because I'd carried through here despite all the difficulties? I could easily have thrown in the towel in those early weeks, or been fired. But I had stuck with it, held on, and was now even seen by my employers as strong and reliable. *She'll listen to you if she'll listen to anyone.* Ironic, wasn't it?

I had even established a life of my own here. A different kind of life, true, but—I'd given this considerable thought lately—would I really want to return to the kind of life I used to have in my marriage? If Oliver and I had stayed together, that would have been another matter. But I had grown away now from the kind of life I had led with Harry, in the same way as I'd grown away from the people I used to know back then. The people Joanna wrote me about had come to seem like strangers met in a distant land, speaking another language. Similarly, I'd begun to feel that whatever I had to tell Joanna about my life here wouldn't be entirely comprehensible to her. Harry, I knew, would describe my friends here as "fringe types." Joanna would know better. Still, Joanna's circle—which had been mine, too—wasn't exactly filled with mavericks. You wouldn't find a Lilly in that crowd, nor a Graham—and certainly not a Jack Fielding as presently constituted, though the earlier Jack, credentialled by wife/children/conventional job, would have fit right in.

Joanna had called after her return from Greece and pressed me again about a visit. "I'm dying to see you. Everyone here keeps asking about you. They all want to see you."

"Yes. But—"

She'd caught my ambivalence. "It'll be just you and me, if that's the way you want it. I won't make any parties or call a lot of people."

She sounded warm and eager, she meant so well, was

such a good friend. But something had changed. Or rather, I had changed. It might be fun to go back for a visit. On the other hand, it might not. Back there, people—perhaps even Joanna—would still view me as an oddity, a pathetic loser cast out of the life for which God, fate, and Harry had intended me.

Eventually I'd told Joanna that I wouldn't be able to visit just now because the situation had changed. "Paula's still here. She hasn't gone back to New York so far. They've separated."

Like Callie, she'd been aghast. "But, Iris, what will you do? I mean, if the house is sold?"

"I'll deal with that when I come to it. I'm not worried, Joanna."

I meant it. The old paralyzing fear had vanished.

Couldn't Callie, here with me now, see that? You may be a hot-shot lawyer, Callie, but I don't think you get the whole picture, even now. Due to a certain inevitable blind spot about one's parents? Beth with Paula, Callie with me? Your children seeing you always with the past superimposed—in the same way as we saw them, perhaps. I wondered suddenly how Callie and Beth would get on, if they ever met. I wished I could somehow bring them together, could hear what they might have to say to each other on the subject.

Callie calmed down and we talked about other things now. She told me about the wedding.

"I must say, it felt strange. Not as bad as I expected, though. Wendy's all right. Hearty. I can just hear her with patients. 'Buck up, little man, right as rain in the morning, hup-hup.' "

So that was what Harry wanted?

"He looks so different," she said.

"Harry?"

"He's grown a moustache, lost some weight, dresses differently."

I felt nothing as Callie told me these things, not the slightest twinge. I only wished Callie could say the same, but that was going to take a while.

"Alistair and I hit it off. He came and sat next to me at dinner. Showed me his matchbox collection. He carries it around with him. Keeps dead bugs in some of them."

The Hunts had been at the dinner, she said. "And the Bidwells and the Raskins and Leila and Art."

And Joanna and Nat? Had they, too, helped celebrate my ex-husband's nuptials?

"They weren't there. I tried calling, but I guess they were out of town, I didn't get them. At the wedding, Janey Ketch came over and asked me about you. She said to give you her love, she often thinks of you."

"Is Wyman still telling those terrible jokes?"

"I don't know. He wasn't in evidence. Janey seemed to be alone. Someone told me they've split."

Which explained why she was thinking about me, no doubt.

"Is there someone in your life, Callie?"

"No one special." She seemed to be trying to decide whether to say more. Finally, she did. "Actually, there *is* someone. I can't count him, though."

"Why not?"

"He's married."

This from *Callie*?

"He's in the firm. Oh, it's got something to do with the fact that we work together. Work well together. There's a certain kind of excitement in that. But I realize—well, never mind." She paused. "His name's Harry, would you believe? Henry, actually, but he's called Harry. He's forty-six." Her tone was very slightly defiant.

All these daughters looking for their fathers. At least she seemed to understand.

"Are you shocked?" she asked.

"No." I resisted the temptation to say, *but surprised, yes.*

"However, keep me in mind as an adverse example," I said, dryly. "Don't rush into anything."

Callie and I were up early next morning. I hoped Paula would sleep late so that we could have breakfast alone. I got lucky: she did. At seven-thirty, we left for the airport, taking an indirect route because I wanted to show Callie something of the coast. At Wixsey Light we left the car briefly and walked out on the headland. Through the mist of early morning, we could make out the sea pounding the pink granite ledges, could look out across the opalescent water to the stepping stones of distant islands.

"It's so different from the Pacific," Callie murmured.

"Yes. That's lovely, too, of course," I said, though in fact I've always thought the Pacific a rather boring ocean.

Above us, something flew. Large head, broad shoulders, long tail, long pointed wings. Was it? Yes!

"Look, Callie! A peregrine falcon!"

Together we watched. "How do you tell?"

"General shape, outline, flight pattern. That peculiar rowing motion as he moves his wings."

Two things you taught me, Oliver: how to recognize birds. And love's fallibility. Should I be grateful for both of those?

"Do you ever think of Wellfleet?" Callie asked.

"Sometimes."

"I always loved it. We always seemed like a happy family when we were there."

So many things I wanted to say, ought to have said, to that. I tried to find the words, but before I could, she spoke. "Alistair will like it, I think. I told him about it. I told him about that place where we used to find sea urchins, remember?"

At the airport we hugged before we parted.

"I want you to come and see me soon. How about Thanksgiving? Will you?"

"Yes. I'll look forward to it, Callie."

"So will I." Another squeeze, then she let me go and picked up her bag. "Take care of yourself."

"You, too, Callie love."

I found Paula dressed, just finished breakfast and putting away her dishes and ours, which I hadn't had time to take care of. "There's some coffee left. Would you like another cup before I empty it?"

"I think I would," I said, and sat down and burst into tears.

She sat down next to me. "I don't know what you did or how you did it, but she certainly is a splendid young woman."

What I did. It seemed to me I'd done everything wrong. Perhaps Harry, indulging her in everything, had been right. Or perhaps it didn't have much to do with us, beyond the years of earliest childhood. Perhaps it was only a matter, after all, of genes and luck, unpredictable fate which blindly apportions.

"Yes. She invited me—"

But I couldn't stop weeping. *We always seemed like a happy family.* Perhaps Alistair would have better luck.

# 16

CALLIE'S VISIT SEEMED to have taken us another step forward. Was this because Paula now knew something of me, through Callie, as I knew something of her through Beth? Whatever the reason, it felt as though our lives had begun to mesh. In more ways than one. A stranger coming into that house might have been hard put to it to tell which of us was the help. Not only did I no longer do floors and windows, but she had begun to work alongside me now. While I ran the vacuum cleaner, she would dust. While I cleaned the stove, she would iron. It came to me that just as I had once found this work a boon, it was now serving the same purpose for her: occupational therapy of a sort. We shared the work now, and the food shopping and errands. We went out together at times to a movie or a meal. Together we conferred over problems of maintenance—of the house, the grounds, the pool, the cars, ourselves. Of such assorted elements was our relationship forged. These, and a shared concern over Beth. At intervals, in the middle of talking about something else, she'd say, "It's been two weeks—" (or three, or four)—"since that call."

"I know." I, too, was counting. "Hang on. It'll be all right."

"Will it?"

"Of course."

I can't say exactly when the change began. I think it started at the time of the Wenzels' picnic, the second Sunday in October. We were all contributing various items: I was bringing salad and muffins.

At noon that Sunday, Paula came in as I was working on the salad.

"Delicious smell."

"Muffins. Want one?"

She shook her head. "Calories. Goodness, what an amount of greens. How many people are there going to be?"

"Eighteen."

"It certainly is a perfect day for a picnic."

Yes. There had been rain lately, but the day was dry though cool, the air sparkled, the sun shone between the scudding clouds. At night and early morning, frost brought its chilly reminder. But the trees still held their fiery glory, and in the fields, asters bloomed, rich purple blossoms centered with gold.

She stood watching as I cut up scallions, sliced tomatoes, measured herbs.

"Have you seen that *Vogue* around? The thick one, the special issue?"

"Upstairs. In your bathroom, I think."

"I think that's what I'll do, curl up with that while you're gone. Why don't you take some of the good bread we got from Jennings?"

"Don't need it, with muffins."

"You can always use good bread. I'll wrap it up for you."

"But, Paula—"

She wrapped the bread in foil, then in a pretty linen napkin.

She pressed on me a bottle of wine.

She brought out a fitted hamper. "Neat, isn't it? Take it along."

"Paula, thank you, but—"

I was beginning to realize. I was also trying to resist realizing.

She wouldn't leave me alone, she stayed right there, hovering and hovering till I thought I'd scream.

Finally, I went upstairs and called Sue and asked if I could bring her along.

"Of course. The more the merrier."

From time to time after that, I began to take her with me, though not with whole-hearted enthusiasm. I didn't mind spending time with her when I was free, but including her in my own arrangements was another matter. For one thing, I needed and wanted a life of my own separate from the time I spent with her. For another, it soon grew clear that my friends weren't altogether pleased when I brought her along. It wasn't hard to see why.

Why was it, I wondered, that when she and I were alone, she was relaxed and natural, but as soon as we were with others, she became affected, tense, and overbearing? It took me a while to find the answer: for her this was the same pattern as in her marriage; she knew her company wasn't sought after, that she was tolerated only as a favor, as part of a package. So, striving for acceptance, she tried too hard to impress. The result was fatal.

At the picnic that day it hardly mattered because there was a crowd. Being outdoors helped too. In that setting, with lots of chatter going on, lots of movement back and forth, any negative impression she might make was diffused. But on other occasions it mattered considerably.

The Benbow gallery, where we had bought *Hijinks*, sent her an invitation to a five o'clock opening of a local painter.

I went with her. There we ran into Alex and Daphne, who had another couple with them, Freda and Woody Brown. Naturally I introduced Paula, who immediately became a lofty patroness of the arts.

"I picked up something here recently by someone named Lobello." It was Lodico, actually. "Quite a nice little picture.

No comparison, of course, with the kind of thing one gets in New York . . ." On and on she went.

I shriveled with embarrassment. Freda and Woody moved away. Alex and Daphne remained stolidly polite, but I could imagine what was going through their minds. Especially Daphne's.

". . . across from the Metropolitan. Oh, the happy hours I've spent there . . ."

A little later Daphne took me aside. "We're going out to dinner from here, with Freda and Woody. Can you ditch that dame and join us?"

I longed to, but I didn't see how. Regretfully I watched them leave, resenting the fact that I was stuck with Paula. "Quite a nice little woman, that Mrs. Jenson," Paula said, as we drove home later.

The following week Paula and I were having lunch out after a morning's errands when who should come into the restaurant but Graham, with Jim Nowell. Graham had been seeing more of Jim since Roy's departure. Jim was older, with soft wrinkled features and hair that was too richly chestnut to be natural.

I excused myself to Paula and went over to say hello.

"So that's her sainted mother, is it?" Graham's voice was a little too loud.

"Graham, hush. I'd better go back now."

"Yes, you'd better. She obviously doesn't approve. Look at her. Anyone would think you were consorting with lepers."

I walked hurriedly away.

"People like that," I heard him tell Jim, "think their money can buy them anything. You should see how her daughter operates."

"More friends?" Paula said brightly. "Goodness, I don't know where you find them all! Would you like to ask them to join us?"

"No, Paula."

"Don't hesitate because of me. I'd be only too glad—"

"I don't want to, Paula."

"Shall we send drinks over?"

"Paula, *leave it alone*. Please."

Next day, on the telephone in the kitchen, I discussed plans to go with Lilly to an estate auction. Paula, all the way in the den, seemed to have overheard. (Could she have been listening on the extension?)

"Is that the Beresford estate?" she asked me afterwards. "I'd be curious to see what kinds of things . . ."

"Absolutely not," Lilly said firmly, when I called her. "Anyway, can you see her riding in the truck with Skoota and us?" If Paula were determined to go, she and I should drive there on our own. Lilly would look for me there, at the preview.

So I went with Paula. We did see Lilly briefly, before the auction started, as she and Skoota moved around looking at the items on display, consulting their list. She nodded at Paula, spoke to me for a moment, then disappeared with Skoota in the crowd.

"Not exactly friendly, is she?"

"She doesn't have time to socialize, Paula. For her, this is business. Look, what a perfect little table . . ."

In the fall sunshine we wandered around looking at Early Tapered Leg Hepplewhite Stand, Pair Mahogany Twin Size Custom Sleigh Beds, Rare Oak Music Cabinet with Slag Glass Panel Door, Marine Sextant with Box, Ogee Mirror. There were linens, jewelry, clothing—a grey cutaway stiff enough with age to stand on its own, a velvet smoking jacket, a man's coat with fur collar, dresses flowered and bugle-beaded, fringed shawls, gloves, boots.

Paula looked troubled. "Sad, isn't it, personal possessions laid out to public view. It seems wrong."

I felt the same way.

She bid for and got the small pine table I'd admired. I couldn't think why she wanted it, it certainly didn't go with the house. I came away with a box of old picture postcards, scenes of the area from the early 1900s.

At the end of the day Lilly and Skoota loaded the truck and left, with no mention of our usual stop for chowder on the way home. Paula and I drove off by ourselves and dined in the almost empty dining room of the Briar Hotel, which would close the following week.

I didn't take her everywhere. I didn't invite her when Lilly asked me over to meet a former college roommate who was visiting. Nor when Jack and I and the Johnsons went to an amateur production of *Kiss me, Kate*, for which Alex had supplied publicity pictures and Daphne had helped make costumes. I stood fast on quite a number of occasions, no matter how pathetically she presented herself.

She watched as I slipped on my jacket one evening on my way out to Graham's.

"What play are you reading tonight."

"*The Master Builder*."

"It must be fun, getting together like that. How many of you?"

"Six. I must dash, Paula, I'm late."

I was about to drive off when she came running out, calling my name. But she only wanted to remind me to be sure to get gas, the tank was almost empty. "Have a good time!" She stood waving as I drove away.

Jack and I went to see *Bringing Up Baby*, the final show before the Regent closed its doors for the winter. As the lights went up afterwards, I thought I caught a glimpse of a familiar figure hurrying out ahead of us. "I think that's Paula!" I told Jack.

"The boss lady?" He peered after her, but already she had gone.

Next morning she said, "I saw you at the movie last night."

"Yes, I saw you too."

1 6 6

"I'd have come over to say hello, but I didn't think I should intrude. I must say, I think your friend looks interesting."

The touch of coy inquiry in her voice set my teeth on edge. "He is," I said, and changed the subject.

Jack grew more and more annoyed because I wouldn't stay overnight.

"Why do you feel an obligation?"

"Not an *obligation*."

"What, then?"

"I'm sorry for her, that's all. She's been through a rough time. And she's nice to me nowadays."

"Why shouldn't she be nice to you? She's lucky to have you. You don't have to carry her around on your back."

"I'm not."

"You certainly are."

It grew into a quarrel. We didn't speak to each other for three days. Then he called and apologized, and I apologized. Peace was restored.

"How about that concert on Saturday?"

"Saturday?" Paula had proposed we go out to dinner. I'd said I was free. "I can't. I promised Ruth—"

"I thought you said Ruth was in Boston this week."

"Well, I—" Why on earth was I lying about this?

"Never mind. Just think about what you're doing, Iris. Just give it some serious thought." He hung up.

I did. And faced at last what I'd begun to know for some time: Jack was right. So was Lilly. So were they all. This couldn't continue. Paula's dependency was coming between me and my life. So long as I let this go on, nothing would change. For either of us.

I had a talk with her.

"You ought to go back to New York, Paula. This place isn't good for you."

She drew herself up. "Where I go and what I do is entirely my business."

"Paula, I'm speaking as your friend, don't you see? You need to be where you can develop your own life and interests—"

"I'll go where and when I feel like going! When I'm ready!" She stalked out.

So long as I was available, she wasn't going to be ready. But *I* was ready. The time had come. In that moment I knew it as surely as though a voice in the wings had given me a cue.

For just an instant I waited cautiously. What came next? Fear? Wavering? A desire to retreat?

Instead I felt a small flutter of anticipation, followed by rising excitement.

I began to read the want ads in earnest. I checked all the area newspapers. I read all the notices at the college. Yvonne would still be away on tour. But I told everyone I knew in the area that I was looking for a job. Everyone promised to be on the lookout.

"About time," Graham said. "Let her find herself another slave."

"Hallelujah," Lilly said. "I'd begun to think it would never happen."

"I'll believe it when I see it," said Jack, darkly.

Ruth undertook to monitor the university publications that listed jobs.

Daphne and Alex said they hoped I'd be staying in the area. "I'm going to try here first," I said. "Then I'll see."

When finally I learned of something, it wasn't through any of my friends. I found the listing in the local paper. *Housekeeper, experienced, year round, full benefits.* At the Staunton Inn.

At first I dismissed the idea. Then I decided there'd be nothing to lose by exploring it. This would be a different kind of housekeeping. A real job. Subservience wouldn't be in the picture.

While Paula was out shopping, I called the Inn and made an appointment for the following week, Friday, November sixth. You'd have thought I'd committed a criminal act, the way my heart pounded.

Shortly after, Paula returned from her shopping trip and showed me what she had bought—a silk shirt, a cashmere scarf, a French fisherman's smock. They were all lovely. Her taste was faultless.

"Do you really like them? Here you are, then." She gave me a package. Inside were duplicates of all these items, in other colors.

"Paula, I can't accept—"

"Try on the smock first. I'm dying to see how it looks."

"But, Paula—"

"With all you do for me, Iris, it's such a small thing for me to do."

What could I do but accept with as good grace as I could manage? But it made me feel low, deceitful, deceptive. Perhaps I'd let that appointment go, after all. Housekeeper, even at a hotel, wasn't anything to write home about. The salary, even with benefits, probably wouldn't equal what I was now making. And I'd need to find a place to live, and what could I find, at a price I could afford, that would be half as comfortable, in as lovely a setting, as my rooms here? And Paula—well, I'd work it out with Paula somehow. Even with her irritating ways, she was all right, really. She had some good qualities. And she was certainly being kind and generous to me these days.

Yes, in some ways there were unique advantages. Looking at it from the outside, many people—Callie notwithstanding—would think I was fortunate.

Yes, perhaps after all I'd ease up on job-hunting for the time being. In any case I shouldn't grab the first thing I saw. Better to delay a while, wait for the right thing to come along.

# 17

AS THOUGH TO MAKE US PAY for the mildness of October, the weather changed abruptly. On the first of November, a north wind began to blow and never seemed to stop. Even the cries of the birds sounded faint against the howling wind. The ocean thrashed and tossed like a feverish patient; the moment of hiatus as the tides changed seemed no longer a peaceful pause but an ominous prelude. Only rarely did a weakling sun emerge from the livid clouds.

Wednesday, November fourth, was Daphne's birthday. Alex was throwing a surprise party for her at Keeler's, a local restaurant. I went shopping for a gift and bought a blue and white cachepot. Jack was making her a marvelous thing, a lacy grille to go in a window.

On the day of the party the weather grew worse. By five o'clock what had begun as a pelting rain became torrential. The radio broadcast high-wind warnings. *Northeast winds of forty to fifty miles per hour with higher gusts may cause considerable tree and power-line damage. Heavy rain and poor visibility will . . .*

"Must you really go out tonight?" Paula demanded. "It's dreadful out there."

I kept an obdurate silence.

She turned up the volume. . . . *marine storm warnings are up along the coast from the Merrimack River to Eastport . . .*

*Winds over the open water are running fifty to sixty knots . . .*
*Tides are running two to four feet above normal . . .*

"There's going to be a hurricane!" She sounded terrified.

"They don't get hurricanes in this part of the world, Paula. You've surely been through this before."

But of course, she hadn't, I realized a second later. In the past she had always been back in New York by now.

Jack was coming to pick me up at six o'clock. Just before six, Paula came out to the hall where I was putting on slicker and boots. "I'm afraid I can't let you take the station wagon out in this, Iris."

"I don't need it. I'm getting a ride."

She watched as I did up my slicker. "You're really going to leave me alone here with this going on?"

Her voice was unsteady. Her eyes were wide and white, like those of a frightened horse.

For a moment I hesitated. Perhaps, after all—But what would I say to Jack? I could imagine what his reaction would be. And Alex and Daphne's. And I'd been looking forward to this.

"Please," Paula said.

Should I?

The doorbell sounded.

"Paula, you're not a child and the house isn't matchwood and there isn't going to be a tidal wave."

We got there more or less on time, but several people were late because of the weather. The road was flooded in places and they'd had to take the long way around the headland. "I thought the wind was going to pick us up and deposit us in the drink at one point," Woody said.

The party really was a surprise. Frank Wenzel was poised with camera to snap Daphne as she came through the door. Daphne at first screamed and clutched her breast, then quickly recovered, swore roundly and threw herself into the party spirit. "Alex, you devil! If I'd known, I'd have put on all my finery!"

"You look very finery to me, my love."

Dinner was delicious. There was champagne. There were countless candles on the cake that was shaped like a horse shoe.

"What a conflagration!" Daphne applied herself energetically to the huffing and puffing necessary to extinguish them.

As we drove home later, Jack had to wrestle the wheel to keep the car on the road. I turned on the radio. . . . *caused by an intensifying low pressure system located southeast of Nantucket Island, moving north to north-northeast passing across New Brunswick or Nova Scotia later tonight . . .*

"Jack, I hate to think of you driving on in this. Why don't you stay at the house tonight, instead of going on to Merriam?"

He hesitated. "Is *she* around?"

"Well, yes, but—"

"I guess I'll go on home, Iris. I want to get an early start tomorrow anyway."

Finally, we were there. Clutching each other, we made it safely to the door. Inside, I stood by the door till I heard the sound of the car driving away.

Paula came hurrying down the stairs. "Thank goodness! I've been so frightened!"

In the car I hadn't found it frightening; there had been something thrilling about being out there in the midst of the elements, while we two were snugly enclosed in the car.

"I think I'll make some tea. Do you want some, Iris?"

I said I'd join her, because I could see she was really in a state. When she poured the water, a little spilled.

"Let me." I took the kettle from her.

Rain beat against the panes. The sound of the wind was the sound of unearthly terror. Was it the sea I heard in the background, a deep low roar that kept going, an endless counterpoint to the screaming gale?

"That dreadful noise!" She put her hands over her ears.

"Why don't you take a pill tonight, Paula? Otherwise you'll lie awake listening." I stood. "I'm going up to bed."

"Wait! I'm coming, too!" She cleared away the cups.

We went up the stairs.

"Sleep down here tonight, Iris, along the hall. The top floor isn't the best place to be, with this going on."

If I stayed down there, she'd come knocking at my door every five minutes. "I'm going up, Paula. Don't worry, I'll leave my door open. I'll hear if you call."

I turned off the lights and stood at my window, but there was nothing to see except blackness. The trees, lashed to frenzy by the wind, creaked and whined like souls in torment. I imagined this wind howling over icy plains, over the endless ocean waters. Were there ships out in this, boats whirling down into the seething depths, sucked down into the greedy troughs forever?

I got into bed, where for a while I lay listening to the tumult. Then I pulled the covers over my head and slept.

*What was that?* An immense, grinding groan, then a huge tearing, rending. Something enormous crashed down overhead—the bed shook as though in an earthquake. I held on, closed my eyes against the sight of the house falling in.

Silence. I opened my eyes. The ceiling was still there. But something had fallen—

For a second I lay paralyzed with terror. Then I got up, ran out of my room, and flipped the switch for the hall light. Nothing. In darkness I groped my way down the stairs. "Paula?" There was an acrid smell, something like dust but not dust, that made me cough. Outside the wind was still howling, it seemed to be blowing right through my nightclothes, why was it so bitterly cold in here?

I opened the door to Paula's room. It opened a foot, then stopped. "Paula?" A giant hand seemed to squeeze my heart. I pushed and pushed. It would open no further. *"Paula? PAULA?"*

"Something fell—" Her voice came faintly. "I'm pinned—"

"Paula, I can't get the door open, something's against it. I'm going downstairs to phone for help, and get a flashlight. I'm coming right back, I'll be right here with you. Do you hear?"

"Yes." Not strong that voice, but she was alive, conscious. Please, let the telephone work.

They came quickly, the rescue squad, ambulance, police. Broke down the door, sawed the limb off the fallen spruce, got her out.

The far wall, where the windows had been, gaped to the elements. The deck was gone. Part of the ceiling was down. A miracle that she was alive, seemed to have no major injuries. "Lucky that bed wasn't two feet further over," the sheriff said.

They took her off to the hospital, wrapped in blankets. I went along. The intern confirmed that her only injuries were minor cuts from broken glass, and a good many contusions and lacerations. "For a while you'll look like a fighter who lost in the fourth round," he said, jolly. "You'll have some aches and pains for a while. Pretty lucky, though. Not even a fracture."

He wanted her to stay overnight, in case of shock. But she wouldn't stay, insisted on going home.

"You'll be with her?" he asked me.

"I will."

He gave me a sedative for her, and the sheriff drove us home.

She wept all the way as we sat together in the back of the car. "Suppose you hadn't been there, Iris. Suppose—"

"Hush, Paula, it's all right, it's over now." I kept my arm around her. "You're all right." Thank God, oh, thank God. I offered up a silent prayer of gratitude.

Back at the house, I made up beds for us on the living-room sofas. They'd said it would be all right to use the upstairs, except for her room, but we weren't going back up there tonight, perhaps not for the next few nights. It was freezing up there, anyway, with that great gash in the wall.

I helped her into pyjamas, then saw her into bed on one of the sofas. "Are you warm enough? How about another blanket?" Pathetic she looked, with those scratches on her face, bandaids over cuts, an elbow bandaged. I fetched another blanket and tucked it around her. "There. You'll sleep now."

She seized my hands, clutched them so tightly I couldn't get free. "Don't leave me, Iris!"

"I'm going to sleep right here—"

"Don't ever leave me, I couldn't manage." Her voice ran on, fast, pleading. "Leo knows I need you. You'll have whatever you want! Stocks, pension, a car of your own, beautiful clothes. We'll travel. Please! I need you, Iris, need—"

"Hush, Paula, go to sleep, everything's all right. Don't worry, I'm right here."

Long after she had fallen asleep, I still lay awake, hearing that voice pleading, begging.

It was an alternative, wasn't it? It would be my job, a full-time career. I would live well, no doubt about it. No further financial worries, now or in the future. But the price? No life apart from her, it would be almost like a kind of marriage. Still, I'd be the one with the upper hand this time. She was the one in need now, I was the one with the power.

# 18

UNTIL I GOT RIGHT UP to it and went inside, I didn't realize how large the Staunton Inn actually was. Mammoth, fronting on the ocean, with long wings on both sides. In the spacious high-ceilinged lobby, with its long polished front desk, there was a post-seasonal catch-your-breath hush, though there were people around who seemed to be guests.

I found my way to an office on the second floor, to see a Mrs. Teasdale. She asked me a few summary questions, then led me downstairs to an office off the lobby, with *Lewis D. Coppard, Manager*, inscribed on the door. Within was a secretary, in whose care I was left to sit and wait while Mrs. Teasdale continued on into the inner sanctum. After a few moments, she emerged, said, "You can go in now, Mrs. Prue," and departed.

Not a single hair on that gleaming cranium.

"Won't you sit down, Mrs.—ah—Prue."

Strange, I wasn't nervous. Because I knew, really, that my chances of getting this job were negligible? Or was it because I didn't really care much about this particular job? House-keeper, after all. Housekeeping in a different context, true— I saw myself with a ring of large keys attached to my belt, chambermaids scurrying hither and yon at my bidding. And full benefits. A lesser salary than I was now receiving, but with those benefits—oh, yes, a step up, in some respects.

Or at least sideways. Still, I could just imagine Callie's reaction if I called and told her I had a new job as—guess what!

I'd wondered this afternoon, before leaving the house (telling Paula I had a dentist's appointment) how I should dress for this interview. Dress down, I'd thought at first, then changed my mind. No more role-playing. They should see me as I was. What they saw was what they'd get, or reject. I put on a heathery wool suit, grey cashmere sweater, discreet gold chain, small gold earrings and pumps. My hair, I knew, was just right. I looked—not glamorous, which would have been unsuitable, but tastefully groomed, highly presentable.

"You've had no hotel experience, Mrs. Prue?"

By rights, his question should have made me quiver. Instead I answered with aplomb, "Not as such. Still, running a sizeable house—my own formerly, as well as my present place of employment—where I've had to put up guests and arrange for rooms and meals and myriad other needs, has certainly given me valuable equivalent experience."

Where was all this coming from? I talked on smoothly, as though I hadn't a nerve in my body, reciting my record as *chatelaine extraordinaire*, a traffic manager scheduling with the greatest of ease.

"I did a considerable amount of entertaining for many years . . . parties for fifty, seventy-five, a hundred . . ." The time Harry received the Jarowslaw Prize. Callie's graduation party. That fund-raiser for the chamber orchestra. "I was constantly putting up my husband's colleagues from here and abroad . . . In my present job I deal with people well known in entertainment and the arts."

He seemed to be listening intently. Occasionally he interrupted to ask a question—nothing for which I couldn't find an answer. I seemed, all at once, to have answers for everything. Nor did I feel afraid of him, as I'd felt afraid of the gorgon at the Boston employment agency.

"Mrs. Prue, let me tell you a little about our operation . . ."

Come to think of it, he looked a bit like my former lawyer. Not that I'd hold that against him. Anyway, in all fairness I had no right to bear a grudge against Jonathan Barley, Esquire. My own fault, all that, if truth be told. He'd tried to caution me, reason with me. Feet nowhere near the ground in those days. All in the past now, Harry, Oliver. Off they walked into the misty distance, faces turned away.

". . . We close the two wings in winter, but we stay fairly well occupied for much of the time. A number of professional and business groups have their meetings here. The National Numismatic Association, for example, will hold its fortieth conference here at the end of the month. There'll be a three-day hospice seminar on the twenty-seventh. Large private parties, dances, weddings, and so forth. Quite a clientele of tourists from abroad too, Europe, Canada . . ."

Why was he telling me all this? Was it possible I was going to get this job after all?

I could see it now, Harry here for a conference. *Here are the extra hangers you wanted, Dr. Prue.* (He never had enough hangers.) Or perhaps it would be *her* conference. *I'll send down an extra blanket right away, Dr. Prue. And how's Alistair?*

"Mrs. Prue, Mrs. Teasdale feels—and I agree—that you wouldn't be right for this job—"

Ah well, so it goes. At least I'd had the interview. The more, the better; rehearsals for the right one eventually, whatever that might be.

"—but I wonder whether you'd be interested in another slot? Our director of guest relations is leaving at the end of the year. Her husband's taken a job in Atlanta, so she's going to work for our Atlanta operation. We're owned now by a chain, Knox-Carlton. We're in most major cities in the east and south, as well as several coastal resorts . . ."

I was so stunned that I almost didn't follow what he was saying.

". . . very specific requirements . . . good appearance and manner, an ability to meet the public, deal with people. I see you speak French." He leaned forward to check the form. "A foreign language is a definite asset . . ."

*But I don't know the first thing about—*

I hadn't actually said it, had I? Apparently not, for he was still talking.

". . . most of our people have degrees in hotel management, but I'm following my intuition here. With this particular job, it's mainly a matter of common sense and intelligence. And, let me add, a good measure of diplomacy."

Somehow I managed to keep control of myself. "Exactly what would my duties be?" How cool and collected I sounded. As though this kind of thing happened to me regularly.

"You'll deal directly with guests, attend to any special requirements. With business and professional groups, for example, you may have to supply secretarial personnel or track down translators at short notice. With tourists, you'll advise on attractions in the area, help them plan day trips, supply guides if necessary, tell them the best spots to go for a picnic or whatever they're looking for. Someone may want to give a special kind of dinner or party here; you'd help devise a theme or plan the menu in conjunction with the staff. By the way, do you know how to run one of these?"

He nodded at the computer on an adjunct desk.

"I do."

"Good. That'll do to start with. When things get quiet out of season, we'll put you to work on the front desk to learn cashiering, our cash register computer system. Very important for a chain operation. You'll have the chance to learn various phases . . ."

On he went while my head whirled. Was this really happening?

"Well, now, if you're interested—"

He paused, an eyebrow raised inquiringly.

Careful now, sound pleased but businesslike, don't overdo, stay calm. Ah, the games we play.

I gave him a smile. "Yes, Mr. Coppard, I certainly am."
"Good. Let's get down to brass tacks then."

I couldn't resist telling my friends right away, though I swore them all to secrecy until such time as I broke the news to Paula. They were all pleased for me. They all seemed to be glad that I'd be staying around here.

Graham's pleasure at my good fortune, however, contained a definite element of spite towards Paula. "Out of her clutches at last! Serve her right!"

"It isn't *like* that, Graham."

"Isn't it? Perennial victim, that's you."

Illogical and unfair, to take out his bitterness about Roy on Paula. Paula, of all people, who wasn't even aware of Roy's existence. But perhaps it was unreasonable to expect logic or fairness of a spurned lover.

I would have to look for an apartment. I would have to see about getting a car. If I wanted to save money towards a car, I was welcome to stay with her for a while, Lilly said; she had plenty of room.

Jack, too, offered me bed and board. I could share the futon for as long as I liked. But it seemed to me that, quite apart from the prospect of that unyielding surface as a nightly event, I needed at least a room to call my own. At Lilly's I'd have a room to myself where I could close the door and be alone when I wished.

But then I received the best offer of all. Ruth had definitely decided to move back to Boston at the end of November. For the cost of heat I could stay in her house right through till next summer if I liked.

The prospect of telling Paula seemed to cast a shadow over all we said and did, though I was the only one aware of it. I must approach this carefully; I must wait for the right moment, then say it in a way that would soften it, make it easier—for both of us.

The days went by. The longer I waited, the harder it grew. I was due to start at the Inn on January third. I must certainly tell her by the first of December, at the latest.

Meanwhile she was engaged and busy. It's an ill wind, I thought, as I watched her consult with builders and painters. The spruce had been cut up and removed. The damage it had caused turned out to be extensive. Roofing, clapboard, plasterwork, windows and frames, wiring and pipes all needed repair and replacement. Repainting would be needed inside and out. The deck outside that room had been totally destroyed.

Beth's room had also suffered some damage, though nothing major; it would need only new windows and some minor replastering and repainting.

"So long as we're at it, I think I'll completely redo Beth's room. And have the floors refinished. Yes, I'll have the floors done and put a Greek *floka* in there. She used to have a fluffy white rug in her room when she was little. She loved it, used to lie down and rub her face against it. It'll remind her—" She looked away.

If I left—when I left—would I ever learn what became of Beth? Of course I would. I'd keep in touch with Paula. I'd call her, we'd meet, the way friends do. I must remember to say that when I finally told her. Though when she heard, she'd probably leave and go back to New York, or somewhere. No matter, we would stay in touch. I wanted to. Not only because of Beth.

Graham announced he was giving a dinner party to celebrate my new job. Just the playreaders, and Ruth—and would I mind if Jim came along?

I told Paula I was going to a party at a friend's that Friday evening.

Involved with plans, samples, swatches, decisions, Paula took it with good grace; there were no subtle remonstrations, veiled hints, or pleading looks. Just after five that evening, she came into the laundry room where I was ironing the dress I planned to wear. "Have you seen those specifications around, Iris?"

"On your desk." I turned off the iron and put the dress on a hanger.

"You know—" She took two steps away from me, as an artist steps back the better to view his creation. "By daylight, that green goes beautifully with your hair and skin, but at night you look better in paler colors. Why don't you wear your velvet pants and your beige silk shirt instead?" The beige shirt was the one she had bought me.

I didn't answer at once. The thought of wearing her gift for this particular occasion made me feel lower than low, a veritable Judas. Still, I knew it would please her, as well as being more becoming. (She was right about that, she was always right about that kind of thing.) So finally I said I would.

She nodded with obvious satisfaction. Suddenly, like a tree gently bowed by the wind, she leaned towards me and kissed my cheek. "While you're off gadding, I'm going to go over those swatches and make some decisions. By the way, I think I'm going to order those Japanese shades. They'd go well here, don't you think?"

So she was in her den, and I was passing through the kitchen on my way upstairs when the telephone rang. I thought it might be Jack, so I picked up at once. So did she, in the den. Our voices, hers and mine, said as one, "Hello?"

Beth's voice said, "Iris?"

# 19

*"BETH!"* We said it together. Hard to say which was Paula's voice, which was mine.

*"Where are you?"* Paula said.

"Iris? Is Iris there? I want—"

"I'm here, Beth."

"Iris, listen—Jesus, do you have to watch me every second?" she said furiously to someone who seemed to be with her. "Iris, they'll let me go, but only if you come and get me."

"Beth?" Paula's voice rose. "What's going on, what—"

"Don't get hysterical! What they want—oh, hell, just a minute, this guy wants to talk to you."

"Mrs. Tanner? My name's Larry Nederland, I'm with the State Department, New York office. I'm a friend of your husband's."

*"Yes? What is it? What's happened?"*

"Your daughter was—ah—in a spot of trouble in London. She was taken into custody. The authorities allowed her to call the embassy there, who called your husband's office here, who put them in touch with your husband in France. I gather he won't be back till Monday. Anyway, things were squared away—temporarily, at any rate—with the British authorities on condition your daughter left the country immediately. They put her on a plane. I met her when she landed here an hour ago. We can only release her into custody of someone who'll be responsible. Leo suggested you or Mrs. Prue—"

"I'll come right away," Paula said. "I'll be on the very next flight—"

"*Iris!*" Beth was on again. "Will you come and get me please, not her? Please?"

"Beth, I—"

"Beth, dear, I'm coming right now—"

"Not you! Iris!"

"Beth, I—"

"I'm telling you, Mother, if you come, I won't go with you! I don't want—"

"Beth, *shut up*," I said. "Let me talk to Mr. Nederland."

Paula called the airport and made a reservation on the six-thirty plane to New York. The last flight back here tonight was ten-five from LaGuardia. She made reservations for two, then pressed money on me and credit cards.

Her face looked grey. "I'll drive you—"

"No need, Paula. I'll drive myself and leave the car at the airport for when we come back tonight." I didn't want her driving home from the airport alone. Not in her present state. "Paula, listen." I stopped for a second in my headlong rush and tried to put matters right. "She didn't mean that the way it sounded. She's afraid to face you, that's all. Because of the jewelry."

It might be true, it might not. I didn't care. I'd have said anything to remove that stricken look, try to ease her pain.

"Don't worry about me. It's not important." A small smile moved around her lips. "Why do they all choose you, I wonder? All those people you know. Marcus. Beth. Leo, too, I suppose, if that popsie hadn't gotten to him first."

I broke the speed limit driving to the airport. Only as it

finally came into view did I remember where I was supposed to be this evening. It was now six-fifteen. If there were time, I'd call Graham before I got on the plane.

There wasn't time. As it was, I barely made it. I'd call from LaGuardia as soon as we landed.

At LaGuardia, I hurried immediately to a telephone. To my relief, I got through at once. "Graham, I'm terribly sorry, there's been a—kind of emergency—" No time to tell him about it now, I'd tell him later.

"I know. I called the house when you didn't turn up. I hear you've gone to collect Her Royal Highness."

"Graham, I'm so sorry, all your lovely arrangements—"

"Always one or the other of them, isn't it, getting in the way, upsetting everyone's plans. Thank goodness you're just about done with that!"

"Graham—" My heart began to race. "You didn't—you didn't tell—"

"I just asked her, nicely mind you, if there was any word about Roy. She said in that voice of hers—you know that voice, when she's speaking to serfs—'I'm sorry, I think you must be mistaken, Mr. Baxter, I don't know anyone by that name.'"

"*Graham, answer me.* Did you tell her I'm quitting?"

A second's pause. "Well, she must know, mustn't she? News gets around."

He had told her. I was sure of it, though I was sure, too, that it hadn't been premeditated, just that he'd let fly when she answered him in that way. He wasn't to know she was telling him the truth; he'd probably thought she was just dismissing him, if not actually keeping something from him.

The cat was out of the bag now, I thought grimly as the cab carried me into Manhattan. No way to fix that. Perhaps it was just as well, in a way. Perhaps I should even be relieved that this task I'd dreaded had been taken out of my hands.

●　●　●

I don't know what I'd expected, exactly, but Beth showed no signs of physical damage. She looked shabby, though. Seedy. In fact really quite dirty, her hair, fingernails, those jeans. But unscathed, apparently. Was Graham right after all? Was she a tough cookie, growing a little tougher with each of these adventures? Or did each of them take a little more away from her?

We made the ten o'clock plane back. She hardly talked at all on the plane. Only when we had landed and were in the car driving back to the house, did she begin to talk, to answer some of my questions.

"Are you really all right, Beth? In . . . good health, I mean?"

"Sure." Her tone was careless.

And Roy, I asked. What about Roy? Where was he?

"Last I saw of him was at Stonehenge."

"Stonehenge?"

"Yeah, that's a scene, once a year. A festival. All the leftover flower children. You can get pretty well whatever you want there. The cops are good, they leave them alone. All kinds of excitement." She grew slightly more animated. "I took a parachute ride."

"You what?"

"Some kids had a jeep, with a parachute. You strap in, take off, they drive a ways, then release you. Up you go. It's like flying, out there on the Plain."

"High?"

"Not very. Forty feet, maybe. Lots of things going on. Roy fit right into that scene. Not me, anymore. I'm getting a little too old."

Too old for ferris wheel? Too old for carnival?

She didn't say where else she had been, what else she'd been doing, or with whom. I decided not to ask any more questions. Not now, anyway. Larry Nederland had taken me aside, told me she'd been picked up in St. James' Park, where she'd been sleeping. "They found some stuff on her. It took some doing, I believe, for Leo to get them to release her."

•     •     •

"Beth, listen—" I had to find out whether my story to Paula about the jewelry had been basically correct. If so, we could put things right. Beth would herself explain why she hadn't wanted Paula to come. And I must tell Beth now what Paula had said: that she didn't care about the jewelry, she had completely forgiven her.

"Tell me about the jewelry, Beth. What happened?"

She began to cry; tears ran down her face in grimy rivulets. She wiped them away with her hand, and kept sniffling like a child. "I didn't know until we were over there. I found one of the rings in his bag. He didn't care, in fact he bragged about it, gave me the whole list, thought it was smart of him. I guess he thought I'd think so, too. Because I'd taken that money. It was too late to do anything, he'd already sold everything except the ring. We had a row about it. He . . . slapped me around. That's a habit he has, I found out. Iris—" she turned to me now—"I don't want to see her, talk to her! I can't hack it after that! Can you get her to leave me alone? Anyway, why should she worry?" A little of her old defiance, that jeering tone. "Dear old Dad'll buy her more. Payola, right?"

She might as well know. "Beth, he's left her."

She seemed to crumble in front of my eyes. "Oh, Jesus. When?"

"About the time you left."

"He's going to marry her, then, that Noelle St. Clair?"

"Yes."

"Perhaps now he'll be satisfied. Now that he's got the kind of daughter he wants. How's she taking it?"

"Your mother? Badly, at first. Better now, though. At least she seems to have acknowledged it, finally."

"Oh, God, Iris, I was so rotten to her on the phone!"

"Never mind, you'll see her soon, you'll put it right. And

Beth, don't worry, she doesn't care about the jewelry, she really doesn't. She'll just be so glad you're here."

Beth was silent for most of the rest of the ride. I filled in the silence with talk, about one thing and another. I told her about the storm and the damage to the house. ". . . Your mother's having quite a good time, I think, getting it in shape."

I told her something about myself, too—though not about the job. That could wait. I told her my life had changed considerably for the better, that I'd been taking a course, had made more friends, was seeing a man.

"A man?" Interest perked her up a little. "Is he nice? Is it serious?"

"Nice, yes. Serious, no."

Quite apart from anything else, how could it be serious with a man who invited you to move in with him, but who had no intention—ever, so far as I could see—of moving out of that house. "I like this arrangement," he'd said. "It gives me everything I want. These people are like family. Better than family, none of the tensions."

None of the responsibility either. A man who'd been married, fathered children who were now adult, was intelligent and personable, but couldn't take, didn't want, any responsibility whatever. Of any kind. Which didn't mean he was lacking necessarily. It might be the right choice—for him. But I had no wish to commit myself to that kind of existence. I couldn't yet say clearly what I did want, but I was at least beginning to know what I didn't. I'd go on seeing Jack, but I wouldn't move in with him there—or elsewhere.

By the time we arrived at the house, it was close to one o'clock.

Paula had done something wonderful: every light in the house was turned on; against the darkness of the surrounding woods, the house shone like a beacon. I half expected her to greet us at the door, but she didn't. It was the right decision. She must have guessed how Beth was feeling. Better to let Beth ease in gradually, take it at her own pace.

Beth kept a little behind me as we entered the house. I felt, rather than saw, her shiver. "Are you cold? I'll turn up the heat."

She gave me a feeble smile. "Guess I'm not used to this weather anymore."

That, and the fact that she was tired and fearful. How could this meeting be less than difficult, after all that had happened?

Paula wasn't downstairs. I went through the lighted rooms one by one, turning off the lights. Paula, too, must be exhausted emotionally as well as physically. She'd have gone to bed, though perhaps she was still awake, waiting.

"Shall we go see if Paula's still awake?" I asked Beth.

She nodded. "I want to tell her—you know."

She took my hand and held it tightly as we went upstairs. Through that touch I could feel her nervousness increase with every step. Of course the house itself was bound to hold certain memories. Just as well that bedroom wasn't in use; Paula had moved down the hall.

I tapped at the door. We could hear the television going in there. . . .*cetacean mammal known as Delphinus delphis, found in abundance in all seas. . .*

"Do you think she can hear us over that?" Beth whispered.

I tapped again.

. . .*common dolphin is six to eight feet long, and is dark brown to black above and . . .*

"Paula?"

. . . *remarkably agile and delights in leaping great heights . . .*

I opened the door. In we went, still holding hands. There she was, fallen asleep while watching, waiting. We went closer.

. . . *no creatures of the ocean have ever been surrounded with more myth and . . .*

The blood rushed to my head with a sound like the sea hurling itself up the beach.

Not asleep. Her eyes were open, fixed, sightless.

# 20

YEARS AGO, I saw a movie that was set in the southwest, the desert. New Mexico, it might have been, or Arizona. There was a house, a luxurious adobe house, built into the rocks, cantilevered, standing in the stillness of the desert. The sun blazed down. The camera's eye showed the interior, all wide spaces and tile floors and walls of glass looking out on the rocks, the saguaro, the spikey yucca. You saw signs of habitation—a table set for a meal, a book lying open, a watch on a bureau, a shirt tossed down. There were Indian rugs, paintings, plants. . .

Then, somewhere in the house, a telephone rang. You heard footsteps as someone went to answer, you heard a voice speak on the telephone, though you couldn't make out the words. Then the camera took you outside again, to the desert.

Suddenly, in total silence, the house blew up. In slow motion the walls were forced outward, the roof blew apart in a thousand pieces, everything rushed silently up to that burning sky. Seconds later, everything that had been the house and its contents came floating silently down in fragments. You saw it all, knew it all—shards of dishes, colored bits of rug, scraps of paper, bowl of a spoon, leg of a chair, fragment of mirror . . . everything slowly, silently floating down, a grotesque snowstorm.

• • •

By the time Leo arrived, I had myself—to outward appearances—in hand. I gather, from what people say, that I behaved calmly and efficiently, all things considered. I had called an ambulance and the police. (Or am I confused? Was that the night the tree fell?) At some point Alex and Daphne came and took Beth and me to stay with them.

Sue Wenzel brought sedatives, Jack made telephone calls, Ruth brought food, Lilly sat and held my hand, while I held Beth's. Throughout, Beth almost never left my side.

Graham came too. The first thing he said was, "You mustn't blame yourself." He spoke very firmly, as though trying to convince himself, too.

Of course, I know that no blame can be attached to any one person. In any case, what use does it serve, to point the finger at Leo or me or Beth? Callie said, when she heard, "She must have been ill." That is what everyone says, more or less; that she was unbalanced, must have been sick all along, though it hadn't been apparent. You can argue it back and forth and round and round as I did, do, am likely to do for a long time to come. Perhaps forever? No. Time passes, after all, eliding, dimming, shading, altering, like the sea wearing down the rocks or grinding shells to form the beach. The time will come, is bound to come, when this will no longer be foremost in my mind, my life. It will fall back, gradually, to the shadows.

Still, it will always be there, somewhere. I will get on with my life, take up that job, and I have no doubt—strange, isn't it?—that I will do well, make a go of it. And who knows what that will lead to? It will lead to something. One thing always leads to another, it's the Third Law of something-or-other, nothing stays the same, events come in chains, there are always consequences, something always leads to something else.

• • •

Leo and I have something in common now. Oh, yes. Leo sat in his study, from which he had taken his files that day and the signed photographs, and held his head in his hands.

He hardly spoke to Beth. They are locked away from each other, those two. For the time being, anyway. I think that will change. I hope. One never knows, after all, what the future holds.

For Beth, it is worst of all, I think. *I never had a chance to tell her.*

What could I say? *I think she knew?* Hardly, in view of what happened. I couldn't say that to Beth any more than I could tell Leo, *She had got over your leaving.* Any more than I can tell myself, convincingly, *It wasn't the fact that you were leaving.* Oh, I can tell myself that, of course, and do, over and over. For all the good it does.

I'm well aware of the given wisdom: only Paula is responsible for what Paula did. None of us can be responsible for anyone else. So no one need feel guilty. Intellectually, I know that. But . . . there is another factor. I had made myself responsible for her before this happened. No, perhaps it was her doing, she wanted me to be, forced me to be, responsible for her. But even if that's true, I saw what was happening, I should have gotten out sooner. But I lingered. Because she needed me, I tell myself. Or because I couldn't help it, I hadn't yet found my way out. Or—and this I only dare peep at very quickly, furtive glances for only a fraction of a second—was it because it suited me to stay? Did I use her predicament for my own purposes, just as Leo used mine for his?

None of us—not Leo, nor Beth, nor I—will ever be quite the same again. We are changed irrevocably. I don't mean lessened, necessarily. Perhaps the opposite. For Beth, I think this may be the fire from which, if she survives the flame, she will emerge tempered, stronger and more compassionate.

Perhaps the sharing of this burden of mutual history will ultimately bring her closer to Leo.

For Leo and me—I don't know. They say no experience is wasted if you learn from it. What do I learn from this? That life will always take you by surprise, just when you think you've worked things out? That for dolphins, *Delphinus delphis,* there is a natural order, but for poor old *homo sapiens,* life is only anarchy and endings?

Leo wouldn't go into that room. Beth and I packed up Paula's clothing and personal possessions.

Leo said to me quietly, "Her jewelry goes to Beth. Let me have it, I'll put it safely in the bank till she's up to handling it."

I gave him the box. "There it is."

He opened the box. "Where's the rest?"

"That's all I found."

"You looked everywhere?"

"Yes. Go see for yourself."

His eyes fixed on me. "She's had it already, then."

"Had—?"

"Paula must have given it to her, piece by piece, each time she came begging. Or sold it and given her the money."

"If I were you, I wouldn't mention it to Beth. She's in no condition—"

"I know. I won't say anything." He sounded resigned. "What's the difference now anyway? Let it go."

Yes, let it go. Let it all go. If only we could.

"I'm probably going to put the house on the market. I've talked to the builders, they can finish up here in a week or two. The deck will have to wait till spring." So far as the contents were concerned, Beth had said she might want some things. Was there anything I'd like? Leo asked.

I thought.

"Yes. The picture in the front hall. And—there's a small pine table in my living room . . ."

*You're right, Iris.* She'd stood it against my living room wall. *It's charming. And fits perfectly there, don't you think? But, Paula, you shouldn't—*
*Why shouldn't I? It gives me pleasure.*

What would happen to everything else, I asked Leo.
"I'm handing it over to Castleman."
The auctioneer. So now it would be Paula's possessions that were exposed to public view. Some dealer in the crowd would thoughtfully consider the tall, crystal candlesticks that had marched in regimental splendor along the dining-room table. *6 Candleholders, Baccarat, Very Fine.* Some stranger would carry off boxes containing the Creuset saucepans, square white dishes, Swedish stainless cutlery—*Lots 5, 6 & 7, Ovenware, Flatware, Dishes. Excellent Condition*—everything I had used and washed and dried a thousand times.
Not her clothing, though, or anything personal. Beth and I would see to that.
What would Beth do now, I asked Leo.
"I don't really know." He paced back and forth. "She's so—bereft, so—" For a second, he covered his eyes with his hand. Then he sat. "I've been trying to think what I can do for her. She'll always see me as the villain, I suppose."
"No more than she sees herself. Or I see myself."
For a long moment he said nothing.
"Well. She'll come and stay with me, I guess. With Noelle and me. She can't be alone."
He was right about that, she couldn't be. Not for a while. How would it work, though, with Leo and his new bride?
He was saying something, I'd missed some of it. "What did you say?"
Those eyes were on me, the gaze which missed nothing, deduced everything from the merest quiver or eye contact or intake of breath. ". . . If you'd drop that and stay on here and keep Beth with you, I'd make it worth your while. . ." He recited it all, a long list, touching all bases.

"Or, if you'd rather, I'll get you both an apartment in New York or wherever. She's extremely fond of you. You know that, don't you?"

"Yes."

"You'll consider it then?"

"No."

"Are you sure? Give it some thought."

"No. I'm sure."

I understand a good deal more now, about everything. I know now why I took this job in the first place, when I was so desperate. I took it because working here in this house as a servant was so far removed from my normal experience that I could class it as a whim, a masquerade—or, as Callie said, a game. As opposed to, say, clerking at Filene's, which would have been a little too close to the real thing to be laughed off. All this time, I'd been living in a fantasy, a game of let's pretend.

No more.

Remember that television program from years ago? *This— is YOUR LIFE!* My feet are not only on the ground now, they are sunk deep, rooted in cement, it feels like. There is no question now of not facing facts. I will leave this house behind, but this, Paula's death, I cannot leave. It is a fact. It is reality.

Soon I'll be going out to the Coast to spend Thanksgiving with Callie. She has been sweet, loving, and kind. But when I first called to tell her what had happened, she was shocked and concerned, of course, but also—I could tell—worried on another score. I guessed her thought: did this mean that, unemployed once more, I would be going there on an open-ended visit?

I told her then about the new job. She was relieved, needless to say, and very glad for me. She urged me then to plan to stay longer, for a week or two after Thanksgiving.

I probably will, because once I start my job, I won't have time for travel.

I'm looking forward to seeing Callie. I try to fix my mind on that. The brain, they tell me, can't hold two thoughts simultaneously, so I try to keep it filled with topics that aren't troublesome. Thoughts that bring pleasure. The visit to Callie. Lunch with Ruth to go over matters of house maintenance. The kind of car I'm going to buy. The glowing references Leo and Marcus gave me.

Despite everything, I look forward to coming back to Maine after the holiday and starting my job. (There are beginnings as well as endings. I must keep that in mind.) There will be places I have to pass—Corniche, Annabelle's, Maurice, certain restaurants, Bert's PX where we bought *The Times*—which are bound to evoke memories. But the Inn and Ruth's house are both located in the opposite direction from the point, the cove, the house. I need never see the house again, unless I choose to make a detour. Anyway, I won't be here forever.